A Script for Danger

Read all the mysteries in the
NANCY DREW DIARIES

❧

Nancy Drew

DIARIES™

A Script for Danger

#10

CAROLYN KEENE

Aladdin

NEW YORK   LONDON   TORONTO   SYDNEY   NEW DELHI

ALADDIN

An imprint of Simon & Schuster Children's Publishing Division
1230 Avenue of the Americas, New York, NY 10020
First Aladdin paperback edition September 2015
Text copyright © 2015 by Simon & Schuster, Inc.
Cover illustration copyright © 2015 by Erin McGuire
Also available in an Aladdin hardcover edition.
All rights reserved, including the right of reproduction in whole or in part in any form.
ALADDIN is a trademark of Simon & Schuster, Inc., and related logo
is a registered trademark of Simon & Schuster, Inc.
NANCY DREW, NANCY DREW DIARIES, and related logo are
trademarks of Simon & Schuster, Inc.
For information about special discounts for bulk purchases, please contact
Simon & Schuster Special Sales at 1-866-506-1949 or business@simonandschuster.com.
The Simon & Schuster Speakers Bureau can bring authors to your live event.
For more information or to book an event contact the Simon & Schuster Speakers Bureau
at 1-866-248-3049 or visit our website at www.simonspeakers.com.
Cover designed by Karin Paprocki
Interior designed by Mike Rosamilia
The text of this book was set in Adobe Caslon Pro.
Manufactured in the United States of America 0616 OFF
4 6 8 10 9 7 5 3
Library of Congress Control Number 2015943198
ISBN 978-1-4814-3811-7 (hc)
ISBN 978-1-4814-3810-0 (pbk)
ISBN 978-1-4814-3812-4 (eBook)

Contents

Dear Diary,

A FEW MONTHS AGO, THE *RIVER HEIGHTS* *Bugle* announced that Alex Burgess, an exciting new director, was shooting a film in River Heights—starring Brian Newsome! Since then, everyone has been buzzing about how thrilling it is to have one of Hollywood's biggest stars in our little Midwestern town (especially Bess, of course).

I've always thought it would be fun to visit a movie set—the actors, the costumes, and watching a story come to life. I never imagined that most of the drama would be *behind* the camera . . .

CHAPTER ONE

Action on the Set

"I THINK I'M GOING TO FAINT."

Bess Marvin, my best friend, lifted up her sunglasses and surveyed the scene in front of us. It was a hot morning in late June and we had just arrived at the River Heights train station, which was filled with giant trucks, trailers, and a few dozen spectators, all waiting as anxiously as we were.

"He's just a person!" snorted George Fayne, my *other* best friend and Bess's cousin. Although she and Bess are related, they are complete opposites. Take their outfits this morning: Bess was dressed in an elegant blue wrap dress with intricate embroidery along the neckline. Her hair curled softly around her face, and she was wearing just the right amount of mascara to make her lashes look "natural but flirty," according to her. George, on the other hand, was not pleased about getting up so early and could barely be bothered to throw on a pair of cutoff jean shorts and a faded T-shirt that had been through one too many spin cycles.

"Ned texted me to say that he saved us a good spot," I said, shepherding my friends through the small but eager crowd in the parking lot. Many people were holding signs that read BRIAN, I LOVE YOU! and RIVER HEIGHTS WELCOMES BRIAN NEWSOME!

Although I wasn't as starstruck as Bess, I certainly felt like this was a special moment—a real film crew was about to start shooting a movie in River Heights. The director, Alex Burgess, had worked in my dad's law office before pursuing his dream of directing films. Neither my dad nor I were surprised when Alex made the move to Los Angeles. Although he had been a diligent paralegal, he'd always been obsessed with movies.

Alex had struggled at first, working in a diner while writing the screenplay for his film *The Hamilton Inn*. His sacrifices had paid off, though, and now here he was, ready to bring his story to the silver screen.

But it wasn't Alex the crowd had come to see; it was the star of his film, Brian Newsome, who played a handsome doctor on the hit television drama *Hospital Tales*. As my friends and I made our way through the shrieking fans, I noticed that many of the girls in the crowd were dressed as nicely as Bess was.

"Nancy! Over here!"

My boyfriend, Ned Nickerson, stood at the front of the crowd with a camera around his neck; he freelances as a part-time photographer for the *River Heights Bugle*.

Bess barely said hello to Ned, craning her neck toward the side of the parking lot. "Have you seen him yet?"

Ned smiled. "Brian should be here in about fifteen minutes, Bess."

I caught George rolling her eyes and grinned. George usually has little patience for Bess's celebrity crushes.

"Nancy, I cannot believe you know the director of an actual movie! This is *so cool!*" Bess continued.

I nodded, adding, "It's really generous of Alex to invite us here to see the set!"

George yawned. "Why is the coffee cart closed?" she grumbled. Besides not being a morning person, she also hated being hungry. The combination of the two had turned her into a full-on grouch.

"Several businesses in and around the train station had to shut down for the day to accommodate the shoot," I explained, "so Alex wanted to do something special for the business owners and employees to thank them. Especially because he's from River Heights."

"So they lose a whole day of business and all they have to show for it is a photograph with some fake doctor?" George snorted.

"Um, *Hospital Tales* is one of the most watched shows on television," Bess snapped, "and Brian Newsome happens to be an amazing actor, *Georgia*."

Everyone knows that the best way to ruffle George's feathers is to call her by her real name, but I jumped in before George could unleash a snarky comeback. "The movie is paying all the businesses too," I said. "And Alex invited a few old River Heights friends to come to today's photo op, like my father and me. He thinks it will be helpful to have familiar faces here."

"We're lucky," Ned agreed, looking up from his camera. "I've heard that most movie sets are closed to the public because of issues with security and sound and—"

"Psycho fans?" George smirked, elbowing Bess, who ignored her.

"They're going to ask everyone to leave the set before they start shooting," I announced.

"Leave where?" Bess asked hopefully. "Where does the set end?"

"Technically 'the set' refers to the area that will be on camera," Ned replied, "but I'm guessing they'll clear out the whole train station and the parking lot, because it's filled with their trucks and trailers. Sorry, Bess."

"So, what's this movie about, anyway?" George asked, yawning again.

"All I know is what I read in the *Bugle*," I said. "It's a mystery about a brother and sister who move back to their hometown to run their family's old, run-down hotel . . . which might be haunted."

Bess added, "Brian Newsome will be playing Dylan Hamilton, and Zoë French is going to be playing his sister, Malika. Zoë's done some television as well as theater and commercials, but the *Hollywood Times* thinks that *The Hamilton Inn* could be her big break."

"I guess those are for the actors, then." I pointed toward the parking lot entrance, where three long white trailers were lined up. One of the trailers had two doors labeled DYLAN and MALIKA. The door to an especially tall trailer was cracked open slightly, and I could see racks of clothes lining the walls. I figured that was the costume trailer.

It was impressive, really: the vehicles, the bright lights, the crew members wheeling crates and trunks of equipment around, the tangle of wires running all over the ground.

"Wow," I said. "Making a movie is a lot more

complicated than pointing a camera and yelling, 'Action!'"

"No kidding," George muttered. "I just wonder how they *feed* all the actors."

Ned grinned. "There are pots of coffee and pastries, George." He pointed to a table covered in breakfast goodies that was set up near the entrance to the train station.

"For *us*?" George's eyes widened with joy.

"That's what I heard!" Ned laughed. "Plus, isn't that Mayor Scarlett chowing down on a bagel over there? She isn't part of the crew."

"If you say so, Ned!" George trotted off happily.

I smiled at Bess. We both knew that the best way to improve George's mood was by promising free food.

As George waited in line for breakfast, I noticed a fortysomething woman in a wide-brimmed straw hat and brightly colored floral pants speaking angrily to Mayor Scarlett. I was toying with the idea of trying to get closer to hear what she was saying when something bumped softly into the side of my head.

"Oops, sorry," a voice apologized.

I turned to see a pale girl in her early twenties holding a metal pole with a professional-looking video camera attached to the top of it. I could barely see her features underneath her heavy, dark-rimmed glasses. A lone wisp of her chestnut-brown hair was visible from underneath a white baseball cap.

I suddenly recognized the girl's face. "Cora? Cora Burgess? Is that you?" I asked.

She nodded, eyeing me suspiciously.

"I'm Nancy Drew, Carson Drew's daughter. Alex used to work for my dad." I stuck out my hand.

She raised her eyebrows in recognition. "Oh, right. Hi, Nancy." After a few seconds of awkward silence, she took my hand in a feeble shake. Cora was Alex's younger sister, and I'd met her a few times when she visited her brother in my dad's office. As I remembered, she hadn't been terribly friendly back then, either.

Just then George returned with a cinnamon roll in one hand and a croissant in the other. "You guys should get over there if you want some. All the good stuff is going fast," she announced.

"No thanks," Cora replied, looking disgusted. "That food has been sitting out since, like, six a.m."

"Hey, as I remember, it was *your* dream to go to film school, Cora," I said, changing the subject.

Cora nodded slowly. "Yeah, I'm in my second year. I'm doing a behind-the-scenes documentary about Alex's movie this summer."

"Wow, that's amazing!" Bess exclaimed, clearly impressed. Before I could introduce my friends, Cora said, "Excuse me, I have to get back to it. Nice to see you, Nancy." She disappeared into the crowd.

"You'd think she'd be more excited about being behind the scenes on a real film set," George remarked. Flaky bits of croissant fell onto her shirt, and she brushed them off.

"Well, it was *her* dream to be a filmmaker." I shrugged. "Maybe she's jealous that her brother just changed careers"—I snapped my fingers—"and is already directing a movie of his own."

Ned smiled and patted my shoulder affectionately. "That's our Nancy," he chuckled. "Always looking for motives, even when there's no mystery."

Bess and George smirked. It's true that I have a knack for sleuthing. My friends like to tease me about it sometimes, but when I'm working on a case, they're always right by my side. Together we've solved more than a few big mysteries.

"Oh! There he is!" Bess's excited shriek was nearly drowned out by a chorus of others. A black town car pulled up next to one of the trailers, and Brian Newsome stepped out. I could see why he was so popular. His dark-brown hair waved perfectly over his strong, square forehead. His sharp blue eyes had a friendly glint as he smiled, revealing a row of gleaming white teeth. Ned ducked in front of the crowd to get photographs.

Bess jumped up and down, practically hyperventilating. "I can't believe Brian Newsome is in River Heights right now!" she squealed. "I have to get his autograph and a picture of him and a handshake!" She hurried off behind Ned.

"We might need a medic for that one," I joked to George, who shook her head.

"He's just a *person*," she repeated, "although, I guess he is cute in a famous-movie-star-kind of way."

Moments later a blue sedan pulled into the parking lot and Alex, the director, got out of the passenger seat. He looked exactly as I remembered him: tall and skinny, with hazel eyes and stick-straight brown hair that seemed to be growing in every which way. He was wearing a plaid shirt, dark jeans, and tennis shoes. The driver of the car, a caramel-haired, big-eyed woman in her thirties, walked beside Alex. She was wearing black jeans, a black T-shirt, and black sneakers, and she had a serious expression on her face. Finally a tiny, stunning young woman emerged from the backseat. She had the longest, curliest dark hair I'd ever seen, with olive skin and deep dimples in her cheeks. She was dressed in a ruffled blouse with jeans, accessorized with worn cowboy boots and a tangle of silver necklaces. Nobody paid much attention to this trio, however. All eyes were on Brian as he happily posed for photos with excited fans.

Even Mayor Scarlett was among the people who had collected around the television star. "It is such an honor to have an actor of your caliber in our small town," she gushed.

Brian looked at her like it was the nicest thing anyone had ever said to him.

"It's an honor to be here, Mayor Scarlett. When I read Alex's script, I knew I had to be a part of it. I even turned down the lead role in the *Blue Ranger* film because their shooting schedules overlapped."

I raised my eyebrows at George, who, as usual, was glued to her smartphone. "What *Blue Ranger* film?" I whispered. She frantically typed on her touchscreen.

"A huge superhero movie that's going to start filming in a month," she replied after a few seconds. "It's based on a comic book, and apparently the budget is"—George almost choked on the words—"two hundred million!"

Brian stood before his adoring crowd and announced, "Thank you all so much for coming. I have to step into my trailer for a moment, but I hope to have the chance to meet each of you in the coming days." He walked toward the trailer labeled DYLAN before anyone, including Bess, could get an autograph. She came back to stand with us, dejected.

"I was so close!" she cried.

"Don't worry," I comforted her. "I'm sure Alex can make it happen."

Right at that moment, Alex noticed us and started waving. "Nancy! Hey, thanks for coming." He ran over and grabbed my hand excitedly.

"Hi, Alex," I replied, shaking firmly. "These are my friends Bess and George, and my boyfriend, Ned, is over there taking photos. My dad really wanted to be here, but he got stuck in a deposition this morning."

"Oh, that's fine. I know how it gets with Carson." Alex winked. "Anyway, stick around and I'll introduce you to Brian later; he's really nice."

The woman in black pulled him away toward a podium. I caught Bess's eye, which looked like it was about to pop out of its socket at the mention of having an actual conversation with Brian.

Meanwhile, Cora had repositioned herself and was standing next to me again, fiddling with her camera.

"Who's that?" I asked, gesturing toward the woman in black. Cora glanced up. "Oh, that's Lali. She's the producer."

George's ears perked up. "I've always wondered what a movie producer actually *does*."

"Lali does everything," Cora replied. "She gave Alex notes on his script, made the budget, found the investors, and negotiated all the contracts. It's her job to make the director's vision a reality from beginning to end."

George digested this information and asked, "So Alex decides how he wants the movie to look and feel and Lali makes it happen?"

Cora nodded. "Within reason, of course. But Lali's been doing this for years. Alex is lucky to have someone like her on his first film. You know, because he's still so green." She made a face and ambled away.

After she had gone, George said, "The only person who seems green to me is Cora. Green with envy."

Bess nodded. "You might be right about her, Nancy."

A loud whistle silenced everyone, and a high-pitched female voice rose from the front of the crowd. "Hi, everybody!" An Indian girl in skinny jeans with her dark hair piled on top of her head stood on a black wooden box, brandishing a bullhorn. She was wearing a plain T-shirt and cargo pants, with a headset strapped on her head.

"I'm Nysa, the first assistant director for *The Hamilton Inn*," she boomed. "We're going to arrange a formal photo for the *Bugle*, so everyone please move to one side, okay?"

Nysa walked over to the food table, where a grizzly-looking man in his sixties was refilling the coffee machine, replenishing the pastries, and laying out an assortment of other snacks. He was dressed in a khaki vest and sun hat that made him look like he was about to go fishing.

"Sal, I'm going to need you to move craft services over to the other side of the lot," Nysa instructed.

"Are you kidding me, Nysa? This is where you told

me to put it. You want it moved, you move it!" Sal's loud voice and harsh tone caught the attention of several bystanders.

"Why does it always have to be like this with you, Sal?" Nysa sighed, and a young man in his twenties came to help her move the table. I noticed that the man—probably an assistant—was formally dressed in a pressed white shirt and khakis, which made him stand out from the T-shirt-and-jeans-clad members of the crew.

"Be careful!" Sal groaned. "You better not break anything!"

"Wow. Someone sure woke up on the wrong side of the bed," Bess observed as Sal threw up his hands and marched away angrily, disappearing somewhere behind the trailers.

Alex stood in front of the crowd and spoke into a microphone. "Our producer, Lali, and I would like to thank the citizens of River Heights who have been so supportive of *The Hamilton Inn*. We're pretty stoked to be working in my hometown."

Everyone cheered. Lali took the microphone from

him to say, "I'd especially like to thank Mayor Scarlett for allowing us to film here." The mayor beamed as she stepped forward and stood next to Alex.

I suddenly heard sharp tones and a scuffle behind where we were standing, right in front of the trailer housing the bathrooms.

"I don't have time for that right now!" I turned around to see Brian speaking sharply to the well-dressed man who'd helped move Sal's table. George noticed too and threw me a quizzical look. Brian had lowered his voice to an angry grumble, so it was impossible to hear what he was saying, but his body language indicated that they were still arguing.

Meanwhile, Alex invited the curly-haired actress to stand next to him. "This is Zoë French, the costar of *The Hamilton Inn*," he said proudly. "She's going to be a big deal one day, so get a picture now before she's on every magazine cover!"

Zoë stood with poise. "Thanks, Alex," she said. "I'm really proud to be a part of this."

Alex continued, "And finally, the star of our

film. You all know him from *Hospital Tales* . . . Brian Newsome! Where are you, Brian?" Alex searched for his lead actor, who finally emerged from the back of the crowd, beaming. Brian joined the rest of the crew and Mayor Scarlett as they posed for the cameras.

Just as the camera flashes started to go off, a hissing noise echoed throughout the parking lot. It seemed to be coming from behind a truck that was parked right next to Alex, the mayor, and the actors.

Before anyone could react, a deafening explosion ripped through the air.

CHAPTER TWO

~

Snap, Crackle, Pop!

SCREAMS COULD BE HEARD ABOVE THE crackling and popping noises. Brian lunged and draped his arms over Zoë and Lali, pulling them down protectively.

"Everyone get down!" someone shouted.

Bess, George, and I huddled on the cement.

As soon as the noises stopped and we shakily stood up, I saw Lali spring to her feet. A dark-haired man in a black fleece vest and a tool belt jogged toward the truck where the sounds had come from.

"Spencer, be careful!" Lali called after him.

I looked around at the shocked faces of the crowd. Ned rushed over to us.

"Are you guys okay?" he asked.

I nodded.

"That was really scary," Bess whispered, shivering.

"I know," I replied. Even though my years of sleuthing have put me in more than a few dangerous situations, it never gets any easier.

"Everyone all right over here?" Nysa was moving through the crowd.

"Yeah, we're fine," I told her. "Did anyone get hurt?" As I brushed myself off, I noticed that the crowd was moving closer to the site of the explosion, just as curious as I was.

Nysa shook her head. "I don't think so, thankfully. I'm sure everything's fine, but the gaffer, Spencer— that's a fancy word for an electrician on a film set— went with Lali to check it out. It's safer for all of us to stay put until we know what's going on," she said. I could tell from her voice that she was more rattled than she was letting on.

Moments later, Spencer (the man in the fleece) emerged from behind the truck holding an unplugged coffee machine, which was covered in the burnt remains of . . .

"Fireworks," he announced.

"Someone put fireworks in the coffee machine," Lali called out matter-of-factly, walking up behind him.

Meanwhile, Brian seemed especially concerned about the people around him, making sure Zoë's shirt hadn't been ruined and calming down Mayor Scarlett. Cora stood among the bystanders, capturing the whole scene on camera.

"I thought famous actors were supposed to be self-centered and erratic," George mused.

Bess watched Brian with admiration in her eyes. "Not Brian. He has a reputation for being really generous. He volunteers at a soup kitchen and his dog is a rescue!"

I was barely listening as Bess gushed. Now that I knew everyone was safe, the wheels in my head began to turn. "Why on earth would someone put fireworks in a coffee machine?" I wondered out loud.

"It's a mystery to me," George commented casually—but we locked eyes when she said the word "mystery." Was this a real-life case of sabotage on the set of Alex's film? I wanted to banish the thought from my mind, but my detective instincts had already started to kick in. After cracking so many cases, I've learned to listen to my gut.

Nearby, I heard a voice come over Nysa's walkie-talkie. "Does anyone know where Sal is?"

Nysa pressed a button to respond. "I haven't seen him since we moved his table. You don't think he did this, do you?"

I couldn't help offering some insight. I tapped Nysa on the shoulder. "You know, Cora was filming the whole time." I pointed at Alex's sister. "Maybe she has some footage of the explosion?"

Nysa pressed her glittery pink lips together thoughtfully. "Great idea," she said. "I'm Nysa, by the way. I'm the first assistant director, in case you didn't hear me screaming earlier."

"I'm Nancy Drew, and these are my friends Bess, George, and Ned. I'm an old friend of Alex's."

Nysa nodded gratefully before shoving her way through the crowd to where Cora was filming. "Thanks again, Nancy!" she called over her shoulder.

Meanwhile, Alex took the podium again. "I'd like to apologize for the shock, everyone. It appears that this was just a harmless prank."

Most of the crowd, dazed by all the chaos, started to leave.

"Thank you again for supporting our film," Alex proclaimed sincerely. "Maybe the ghosts of the Hamilton Inn are trying to tell us to get to work!" He laughed weakly at his own joke, but his somber expression revealed how much the incident had upset him.

As the crowd trickled out of the parking lot, Ned packed up his camera. "I have to get back to the office and turn in these photos, Nance. They asked me to shoot a piece on the Fourth of July carnival next." The annual Fourth of July carnival was one of River Heights' biggest events. He kissed me on the cheek. "I would offer you a ride, but I know you'd never abandon a crime scene."

I half smiled at how well Ned knew me. "I'm just worried about Alex," I replied.

"Let me know how it goes. I'll call you tonight." Ned patted my shoulder affectionately before darting off.

"Alex does look overwhelmed," Bess observed. "Should we go see if he needs any help?"

I was thinking the same thing. As Bess, George, and I made our way over to him, I heard Mayor Scarlett speaking to someone walking alongside her. I only caught the tail end of their conversation.

". . . it worries me. Maybe Roberta Ely was right," the mayor muttered.

Before I could wonder who that was, Lali's voice boomed out, "Come on, people! Time costs money, and we don't have much of either!"

The crew was like a machine with hundreds of different moving parts. Each person seemed to know exactly what his or her job entailed and how it fit into the bigger picture. Right now, people were hustling to set up lights around the train station's entryway. A circle of crew members surrounded Alex, firing questions at him from every direction:

"The darker jeans don't fit her. How about the blue leggings instead?"

"I don't know if that angle is going to look the way it does in the storyboards. What do you think about changing the lens?"

"Do we really need *two* close-ups?"

As soon as he saw us approaching, though, Alex broke apart from the group.

"Nancy! I was just about to call you to make sure you didn't leave," he said breathlessly. He motioned for us to join him a few feet away from the train station.

"I can't believe that fireworks stunt," he said, keeping his voice low. "Did people seem really freaked out?"

"It was startling," I said, choosing my words carefully so as not to upset him even more, "but everyone calmed down once it became clear that nobody was hurt."

Just then Lali came over and glanced at Bess, George, and me. "Alex, can we talk?"

"Sure. Lali, this is Nancy. She's Carson Drew's daughter, you know, my old boss? And these are her friends George and Bess."

Lali smiled stiffly, her mind clearly on other things. "Nice to meet you. Alex, I need to talk to you about what just happened."

"Any idea who did it?" he asked.

Lali shifted her eyes. "Well, Sal didn't seem to be around when the firecrackers went off, so he has no clue as to who might have been tampering with the machine."

"I noticed that there was some friction between Sal and Nysa," George observed. "Maybe Sal planted the firecrackers to mess with her?"

Lali seemed surprised that we knew so much.

"There's no way," she said. "I've worked with Sal many times, and he can be difficult, but he would never do something like this. He's a professional."

"Are you sure, Lali? He's pretty grumpy," Alex said, suspicion clouding his face.

I could tell that Lali didn't like being challenged,

so I jumped in. "We also noticed Brian having an argument with a younger guy, the nicely dressed one. . . ."

Lali's phone started beeping, and she looked down, distracted.

"Oh, that's Omar, Brian's assistant," Alex explained. "The most devoted assistant in the world. Don't worry; it wasn't him. He would rather die than do anything to mess with Brian's career." Alex rolled his eyes and directed my gaze to Brian's trailer. Omar was juggling a thermos, a coffee mug, and a small grocery bag, trying not to spill anything on his crisp shirt before reaching his boss's door.

Just then Spencer walked by, complaining about a lost pair of wire cutters. "Lali, I'm pretty sure someone was messing around in our truck."

Lali threw up her hands. "We'll put another security guard down there, okay?"

As soon as Spencer was gone, Lali turned to Alex and said, "Maybe we should call the police. We need the crew—and our prankster—to know that we are taking this seriously."

Alex considered this. "I think we should hold off," he replied. "It was probably just some local kids trying to get Brian's attention. We don't want police interrogating the crew, you know? It'll make people uncomfortable."

"I don't know . . ." Lali furrowed her brow.

"What do you think, Nancy?" Alex asked, turning to me. "Is someone trying to hurt us?"

"Not necessarily," I said. "The firecrackers were clearly intended to make a statement. Even the people standing closest to the craft service table didn't get hurt. Did you see the coffee machine? The lid was shut tight."

"She has a point, Lali," Alex agreed.

"Okay, okay," Lali replied, "we'll hold off on the police for now."

I could tell she was still uncertain, but they didn't have much time to discuss it any further because Nysa trotted over to say, "Okay, Alex, we're ready to block the scene now."

Alex invited us to stick around and watch the first shot, which of course drew squeals of excitement from Bess.

As we followed him toward the train station, Nysa caught up to me.

"Cora won't let anyone see her footage," she said, "but she says that she was on the other side of the parking lot the whole time, so all she got was the crowd's reaction. Any other ideas?"

"Nope, haven't heard much," I told her, smiling weakly. I didn't want to share too much with Nysa at this point; it was too early to rule anyone out as a suspect.

"Well, let me know if you think of anything, okay?" she said.

After she had walked away, I turned to my friends. "Don't you think it's strange that Cora won't let anyone look at her footage?" I asked.

"What are you saying? You think she did it, Nancy?" George asked.

"Well, she certainly has a motive—jealousy—and she had plenty of opportunities to put the fireworks in the coffee machine." I chewed my lip.

"No way," Bess insisted. "Siblings may fight, but

they don't try to scare each other half to death! Plus, plenty of people could have planted those fireworks."

"I suppose so," I mused. "Cora was one of the few people on the crew who had a specific task during the reception. She wouldn't have had time to plant the fireworks, light them, and then make it all the way to the podium to get the photo op."

"The suspect could have taken advantage of the fact that most of the crowd was focused on Brian," George added. "By the way, Bess, I think your shrieking damaged my hearing permanently."

Bess didn't have a chance to come back with a witty retort, because another loud scream reverberated throughout the parking lot.

It soon became clear that the sound had come from the costume trailer. As we gathered around, a petite, dark-skinned girl with long braids emerged holding a light green sweater covered in what looked like . . .

"Blood!" Bess gasped.

CHAPTER THREE

❧

Going Undercover

THE GIRL WITH THE BRAIDS SEEMED TO be hyperventilating as Brian emerged from the trailer behind her. I noticed Cora's camera bouncing around nearby. *She sure is diligent*, I thought.

"At the rate things are going, Cora's behind-the-scenes documentary is going to be a horror film," George murmured, raising her eyebrows.

Brian took the sweater and examined the thick red liquid smeared all over it. "Raina"—he nodded toward the girl with the braids—"was just giving me my costume for the first scene; this is how we found it," he explained. I could tell he was trying to look brave. "There's something dripping from the ceiling of the trailer."

Lali, who had run over as soon as she heard the scream, crossed her arms sternly over her chest. "This is ridiculous. Let me get someone to climb up and check—"

Before she could even finish speaking, Brian had managed to get a foothold in the trailer's tiny window and hoist himself onto the roof.

"Brian, no! That's way too risky!" Once Lali realized she couldn't stop him, she grumbled under her breath, "If something happens to him . . ." She cringed as the star crept across the top of the trailer.

"It's fine!" Brian shouted. "Just ketchup." He leaned down to sniff the surface below his feet and added, "Mixed with chocolate syrup?"

The crowd emitted a collective sigh of relief. By the time Brian climbed down, Spencer was inside the trailer, examining a hole in the ceiling. He walked back out, scratching his head.

"It looks like someone ripped a hole up there and poured that stuff down onto Brian's costume, which was on a hanger right below it," Spencer said. "Another prank."

Raina still looked terrified. "Okay. Sorry for all the commotion. I think I have a backup for him."

Brian followed her back into the trailer, while Nysa addressed the rest of the observers. "Okay, everyone, we're already running behind schedule . . . so let's move it!" Everyone quickly went to work, but Alex motioned for George, Bess, and me to come over.

"Maybe I've seen too many movies," he muttered, "but I can't help thinking that someone is trying to sabotage this one."

"It sure looks that way," I replied. "Can you think of anyone who would want to stop the film from happening?"

Alex laughed wryly. "The film business is tough as nails. It's hard for me to think of someone who *wouldn't* want to see this project fall apart."

Lali strode across the parking lot toward us, her

face serious. "Maybe we were wrong not to call the police, Alex," she said. "This is getting creepy."

"No," Alex replied firmly. "The police will only slow down filming by questioning everyone. Plus, getting them involved will draw unwanted attention from the press. That's probably what the saboteur wants. We have to stay one step ahead of him . . . or her."

"Okay, so what do you propose?" Lali asked.

Alex pointed to me. "I think Nancy should stick around and try to figure out what is going on."

Lali's confused expression prompted him to continue. "I trust her. Mysteries are her specialty."

"I know it may sound strange," I offered, "but I've actually been solving cases here in River Heights for years."

"Fine," Lali said. "But no one can find out what you're doing here."

Alex nodded. "Yes. You can go undercover." He paused. "How about the three of you are journalists researching an article about the first movie to be filmed in River Heights." I noticed that his eyes sparkled whenever he was making up a story, no matter how small. "What do you think? You can use your real names, too. The whole crew is from out of town, so nobody knows who you are."

"That makes sense," I said. My friends and I had gone undercover on plenty of cases before.

"Great. Let us know what you find out," Lali replied dismissively. She seemed to be going along with the plan mostly to keep Alex happy.

She then grabbed Alex's shoulders firmly but affectionately. "Now we really have to get rolling. Come on, Alex. Are you psyched?"

Alex rubbed his hands together. "It's time to make a movie!" he exclaimed as he walked off toward Brian's trailer.

Meanwhile, Bess, George, and I hovered near the costume trailer. George's fingers flew across her smartphone as she typed *The Hamilton Inn* into a search engine.

"Alex wasn't kidding about people wanting him to fail," George said. "Look at the comments on this article."

She held out her phone so Bess and I could see what she was looking at: an article on a Hollywood industry website announcing the start of production on *The Hamilton Inn*. While a few of the comments were supportive, several were downright nasty: "I've never heard of this Burgess guy and this idea sounds dumb. Why would anyone finance this?" and "Brian Newsome is a no-talent jerk. Alex Burgess clearly doesn't know what he is doing."

"They're all saying horrible things about people they don't know," Bess noted grimly.

"Because they can do it anonymously," I said, handing George's phone back to her.

"Do you think these comments give us a clue about the suspect?" Bess asked.

George shook her head. "I doubt it. These trolls mostly just like tearing people down with words. I can't imagine one of them going out of his or her way to physically sabotage a movie shoot."

"Okay, so what about Sal?" I asked. "He had the easiest access to the chocolate syrup and the ketchup, as well as the coffee machine."

"But he wasn't around when the firecrackers went off," Bess countered. "Remember? He got all huffy and stormed off."

"Yeah, but maybe he was cutting the hole in the costume trailer while we were all distracted by the fireworks!" George pointed out.

"It's also possible that there is more than one suspect," I added. "For now, let's focus on motive, since any number of people could have rigged one or both stunts."

Just then the costume trailer door opened and Brian and Alex stepped out. Brian looked as handsome as ever in a clean green sweater, distressed jeans, and worn-out work boots. Omar hovered nearby, probably ready to whisk him away somewhere, but Brian stopped to speak to us first.

"Hi, I'm Brian. Alex just told me that you're writing an article about the film."

Bess had suddenly lost the ability to speak, so I offered an introduction. "Yes, I'm Nancy. This is George, and over there is Bess."

"Have you spoken to my publicist?" Brian asked. "Any official interviews with me have to go through her first."

"Our editor will handle it," George said quickly. "For now, we're just taking it all in."

Bess only nodded in agreement.

"It's a crazy business, isn't it?" Brian mused. "When I was in drama school, I had a professor who told me, 'If you can see yourself doing anything else, you should be doing that instead. Making movies is only for people who feel as though they don't have a choice.'" His voice was honey smooth, and his commitment to his craft was undeniable. "Anyway, what are your impressions so far?"

"It's been a little more, um, eventful than I expected," George joked, "but the cinnamon buns are top-notch!"

In a more serious tone, I asked, "Aren't you scared, Brian? I mean, first the explosions, then the fake blood."

Brian chuckled. "Nah"—he waved his hand—"probably just some bored kid trying to get attention."

"You've seen this kind of thing before?" I asked. Brian

paused for a moment, as if he were pondering a response.

Omar piped up, "No matter how organized a shoot is, something always goes wrong, huh, Brian?"

"Oh, sure. On every set there's always something," he repeated.

"So you don't think any of this is unusual?" I asked.

Brian raised an eyebrow. "I hope you write a real story about this movie, Nancy, instead of focusing on any dumb pranks," he said quietly.

I wanted to ask if he knew of anyone who might want to harass him, but Omar's walkie-talkie crackled first. "We're ready for a walk-through."

"That's my cue. See you around, girls. Bye, Bess." Brian looked right at her.

As soon as he was out of earshot, George and I turned to Bess, who seemed to be having trouble breathing again.

George poked her. "Are you okay?"

Bess found her voice and choked her words out. "How can you be so *calm*? He's *perfect*."

George, for once, nodded her head amiably. "He's

nice; I'll give you that. Especially when you *talk* to him, right, Nancy?"

Normally I would have joined George in teasing Bess, but right now, I had too much on my mind.

I also noticed that Raina was finally alone in the costume trailer.

"I'm going to try to dig up more about the bloody sweater," I told my friends. "Can you keep an eye out here to see if anything else strange happens?" George and Bess nodded.

I knocked on the trailer door, and when I didn't hear a response, pushed the door open gently. Raina was inside, ironing a shirt, and I noticed that her hands were shaking. She jumped about a foot in the air when she saw me standing there.

"Hi, Raina. Sorry to startle you!" I apologized. "I'm Nancy Drew, a friend of Alex's, and I'm writing an article about the movie. I just wanted to make sure you were all right."

She let out a deep breath.

"I haven't been a costume assistant for that long,"

she confessed. "I've never worked with a star as big as Brian. All this is sort of new to me."

"So did you see anyone unexpected around the trailer before you noticed the blood?" I asked.

Raina shook her head. "Nope. It was just the usual: production assistants, actors, and a few extras. If there aren't any members of the costume department around, we usually lock up the trailer."

"So when do you think someone might have cut the hole and poured the fake blood?" I questioned.

"Well." Raina seemed to think for a moment. "I guess it could have been during the chaos after the fireworks . . . yes!" She seemed to grow more confident. "After the explosion, I ran all the way across the parking lot to see what was going on. That would have been enough time for someone to climb up onto the roof and cut the hole in the ceiling."

That confirmed George's earlier hunch. The person responsible for putting the blood on Brian's costume wasn't in any of the photographs that Ned had taken for the *Bugle*.

Raina added, "You know, I wouldn't have even noticed the fake blood if it hadn't been all over the first costume I pulled." She motioned to the racks of clothing that lined the walls of the trailer.

It was true; if the hole in the ceiling had been slightly to the left or the right, the fake blood would have fallen on one of the other costumes instead of Brian's. And most of those were in plastic garment bags.

"That means that either it's a coincidence, or . . ."

"Or whoever did it knew which costume was coming up first," Raina finished.

I noticed that every single costume was clearly labeled with the scene number, character name, and shoot day. It wouldn't have been that hard to figure out, if someone knew where to look.

Just then Bess popped her head in the trailer door, panting like she'd been running. "Nancy, they're about to start shooting. We should probably get to the set."

The first shot seemed like a prime opportunity for the saboteur to strike again, if he or she was going to. I ducked out of the costume trailer.

"See you later, Raina." She waved meekly, as if she did not want to be left alone.

When George, Bess, and I arrived "on set," which was what everyone was calling the entrance to the train station, Nysa handed us each a copy of today's "sides," which, she explained, are miniature screenplay pages corresponding to the scenes that are going to be filmed each day.

In this particular scene, Zoë and Brian—or should I say, Malika and Dylan, the brother-sister duo—were exiting the train station in their small Midwestern hometown, having just left an exciting life in the big city. Equipment crowded the station's doorway, and there were tape marks on the floor where Zoë and Brian would stand to deliver their lines.

"Jeez, every scene takes so much planning!" Bess observed, reading my thoughts.

"Quiet on set!" Nysa bellowed.

Everyone quickly fell silent. After a series of military-sounding commands, a camera assistant announced, "Scene Four A-One, Shot One, Take One," and slapped a slate. I had never seen someone do that in real life.

"Aaaand . . . ACTION!" Alex belted.

Upon Alex's command, Zoë and Brian walked through the station's doors and spoke lines about how strange it was to be back home.

While the camera rolled, I noticed Lali speaking animatedly with someone near the trailers, but I couldn't quite make out who it was.

"I'm going to see what's going on over there," I whispered to George and Bess, pointing in Lali's direction.

"I'm sure it's nothing. I mean, Lali wouldn't sabotage her own film," Bess said softly. "Why don't you stay and watch?"

I wanted to, but I had to find out who Lali was so heatedly speaking with; it could be a viable suspect.

I made my way back over to the trailers. As I drew closer, I recognized the person who was confronting Lali: the woman in the hat and colorful outfit whom I had seen with Mayor Scarlett before the firecrackers went off.

I hid behind the bathroom trailer and listened to their conversation.

"But Ms. Ely, the mayor has already given us permission to use the River Heights fairgrounds for our big graveyard scene," Lali explained. "The graveyard is going to be very complicated to build and we need at least two days to get it set up. I wish I could help you out, but my hands are tied."

Ms. Ely? I thought. I remembered overhearing the mayor speaking about a Roberta Ely earlier in the day.

"Don't you have any respect for this town? We have the Fourth of July Carnival on those fairgrounds every year! And now we have to relocate to the high school football field because your silly little scene needs to 'set up' on a national holiday!" If smoke could actually come out of nostrils the way it does in cartoons, I was sure that Ms. Ely's nose would look like a steamboat.

"With all due respect, Ms. Ely, a lot of planning goes into our shoot schedule. We just can't change our dates." I was impressed by how collected Lali appeared, considering the number of crises she had already dealt with—and it wasn't even lunchtime.

Ms. Ely, however, did not take this news well. She stormed away from Lali, shouting over her shoulder, "You'll be sorry, Lily Lollipop or whatever your name is! Your days in River Heights are numbered!"

CHAPTER FOUR

An Inside Job

"... AND CUT! I THINK WE'VE GOT IT. Moving on." Alex jumped up from his chair and started talking to the cinematographer. I had been bursting with my news about Roberta Ely for at least a half hour, but I had to wait until the camera had stopped rolling to approach Bess and George. We had quickly learned that even the quietest whisper or footstep was enough to draw a stern stare from Nysa.

"So this Roberta Ely woman actually threatened Lali?" Bess shook her head in disbelief after I updated them.

George said thoughtfully, "It looks like she has a motive for sabotage."

"From what Mayor Scarlett said, this isn't the first time Roberta Ely has been complaining about the film shoot," I added.

"Maybe she got fed up and decided to take matters into her own hands," Bess said.

"So what now?" George asked. The already familiar sound of Nysa calling out, "Quiet on set!" stopped me from answering.

Bess had shifted her focus back to Brian, while I contemplated the next step in our investigation. It definitely seemed like the saboteur wanted his or her pranks to be noticed. Even though I had heard Roberta Ely openly threaten Lali, she didn't quite fit the profile that I was starting to build in my mind. Our suspect had managed to avoid detection while pulling off two major pranks in the midst of dozens of people, which required a certain amount of slyness. And yet from what I had seen, Roberta Ely demanded attention from everyone she met.

I decided to switch gears and try for an "interview" with Sal. He was certainly bitter about something, but was it enough to make him want to sabotage this film? As soon as Nysa yelled, "Cut!" I made my way to the craft service table. George ran after me.

"Where are you going? You can't leave me alone with Brian Newsome's one-person cheerleading squad!"

After I had filled her in on my plan, she fell into step beside me. After all, George wasn't the type to let me venture to the craft service table alone.

When we got there, though, Sal was nowhere to be seen.

"Where is he?" I wondered aloud.

"Didn't you hear them call lunch?" came a gruff voice a few moments later. We turned to see Sal, his signature scowl etched across his face, approaching from behind us. From anyone else, the question would have seemed perfectly innocent, but Sal's tone was downright accusatory.

"Hi there. I'm Nancy," I said confidently, "and this is my friend George. We're writing an article about the film and we wanted to know if you'd be up for answering some questions."

His eyes narrowed. "Why me?" he asked suspiciously.

"We're interested in every aspect of a film set," I riffed.

But Sal wasn't having it. In fact, he only seemed to be getting angrier. "I don't have time for this. Just leave me alone and let me do my job!" he snapped.

At that very moment, Nysa came scuttling toward us. "Hey, Nancy. Alex is looking for you." She eyed Sal. "Sal! Give me back the stapler! We need to assemble tomorrow's call sheets."

"I returned it to the production office," he insisted. "You kids need to stop blaming me for your lack of preparation."

Nysa remained calm. "Cool, thanks. Have a nice day, Sal."

Sal just grunted and wandered away.

"Was Sal being rude to you?" Nysa asked, but didn't even wait for an answer. "Just ignore him. That's what I try to do."

"What's his problem?" I asked. "He seems to really hate being here."

"It's weird," Nysa began, "because I've heard that he accepts every film job he's offered. Either he gets some kind of satisfaction from being mean or he really needs the money."

I considered that. If either of Nysa's guesses were correct, Sal wouldn't be a viable suspect. In order for him to continue torturing people or to keep receiving paychecks, the film shoot would have to continue. It wasn't enough to bump Sal off my radar, but at this point it was more important for me to discuss the case with Alex.

As George and I followed Nysa across the parking lot, I spotted a piece of paper lying on the asphalt and stopped to pick it up.

"What's that?" George inquired.

Nysa stopped and turned around. "Oh, that's a call sheet," she said when she saw the paper in my hand. "It tells you everything about a specific day on set. What time everyone has to be there, what scenes we're shooting, which actors are involved, how many extras we need."

George peered over my shoulder. "You make one of these every day?"

Nysa nodded. "Well, not me, personally, but someone on my team does. Every crew member gets one for the following day before he or she leaves the set."

"Can I keep this one?" I asked.

Nysa nodded, then led us to the lawn behind the train station, where several picnic tables had been set up in the middle of a vast buffet. A pair of tents protected the food and the crew from the hot sun.

"All right, girls, catch you later!" Nysa exclaimed before rushing off, barking commands into her walkie-talkie.

George eagerly got in line for food, her eyes gleaming. Bess joined us seconds later.

"Where have you guys been?!" she exclaimed. "You missed an amazing performance from Brian."

"Oh, you know," I replied, trying to sound as vague

as possible in the presence of so many unknown ears, "just poking around."

As we served ourselves pasta, potatoes, vegetables, and meat from large trays, I carefully observed the various crew members, thinking about the lengthy list on the back of Nysa's call sheet. There had been at least one hundred people on there, not including the extras, security guards, and reception guests. We might have identified a few potential suspects, but we hadn't even interacted with most of the cast and crew.

When George finally joined Bess and me, her plate was piled at least six inches high.

"You're like a bottomless pit!" Bess cried.

Alex beckoned us to his table at the edge of the tent, and we hurried over to join him. Brian sat across from Alex, while Cora was perched on the edge of the bench, fiddling with some settings on her camera.

"Have a seat, girls!" Alex offered.

George plopped down and promptly began eating her turkey burger. I put my tray down next to hers, but Bess just stood frozen in place, staring at Brian. He was drinking some kind of green, lumpy liquid from a clear thermos.

"Bess, come on!" I called, suppressing a smile. "You can squeeze in next to me."

"Hey, Cora, you'd better give me copies of all this footage you're taking, okay? I'll give you my e-mail," Brian said.

Cora beamed. "Absolutely, Brian!"

I raised an eyebrow in George's direction as if to say, *oh, so Brian can see her footage, but nobody else can!*

"Whoa, guys. I don't want any behind-the-scenes stuff out there yet!" Alex exclaimed.

"*Obviously*, Alex," Cora replied defiantly. "Brian meant after the shoot, right?"

"Of course," Brian said. He finished his green drink. "I'm all done . . . you can have my seat." He stood up and gave Bess a friendly nod. "I have to go over my lines, anyway."

"Um. Thank you?" Bess responded breathlessly.

Just as she sat down, I noticed that Brian had left something behind: a copy of *The Hamilton Inn* screenplay with his name printed in black ink on the cover page. There was a comic book sticking out of it, and I could see the words *No. 1 of the Blue Ranger Series* printed in one corner. I tried to get a closer look, but a hand quickly moved in and scooped up the script.

"There it is! I was so worried." I recognized the anxious, well-dressed young man I'd seen hanging around Brian earlier.

"You're Omar, right?" I asked, and introduced myself.

He nodded, keeping one eye on his phone. "Omar Billings. I'm Brian's assistant. Oh! That, too." He grabbed the empty thermos with his free hand.

"What is that green goop, anyway?" George asked.

"It's a kale-bee-pollen-oatmeal-flax smoothie!" Omar snapped, as if it were the most common thing in the world. "Brian says these help him stay fit and focused."

Alex swallowed a bite of his hamburger. "I keep telling Brian that he doesn't need to bulk up for this role; his character is just supposed to be a regular guy!

But he insists on looking like a movie star anyway."

Omar seemed to take Alex's comment as criticism. "He *is* a movie star!" he fired back. "What do you expect?"

Before Alex could respond, Omar's phone started buzzing. He leaped to attention and hurried off toward Brian's trailer.

"I need a new memory card," Cora announced brusquely, and flounced away.

As soon as we were alone, Alex leaned in. "So, any news? What's the latest?"

"Well," I replied slowly, "Sal is bitter enough to want to hurt people. We haven't ruled him out, but whoever climbed to the top of that trailer and cut that hole had to have been less . . ."

"Old," George finished.

Bess shot her a glare.

"What?" George exclaimed defensively. "It's true!"

"Can you think of any reason that Sal might want to sabotage the film?" I continued.

Alex shook his head. "Not really. I've never even

worked with him before, though. Lali has, but she's one of the few people he's *not* mean to. I can't imagine why he'd want to hurt her."

"What about Roberta Ely?" Bess asked. "That cranky woman who runs the River Heights Fourth of July Carnival? She doesn't seem too happy about you guys shooting on the fairgrounds."

"Would she have gotten a call sheet, Alex?" I asked.

Alex looked momentarily impressed at my use of the proper terminology. "We only give them to crew members, but people leave them lying around all the time, so it's possible." He paused. "But even if Roberta Ely managed to pick up a call sheet, she wouldn't have gotten it till this morning; we sent them out late last night."

"Whoever dumped the fake blood on Brian's shirt would have had to know what he would be wearing in the first scene. That means it's someone who had access to inside information about the film beforehand," I explained.

"Interesting," Alex replied. "So the prankster

is probably a member of our crew! Kind of a creepy thought."

I was trying to figure out the most delicate way to ask Alex about Cora when Nysa shouted, "We're back in!" and, with her army of production assistants, hustled everyone back to work.

"Let's continue this later," Alex said, grabbing his folders and rushing off. Seeing his worried face made me more determined than ever to solve this mystery, but I knew how disappointed Alex would be if Cora was indeed our culprit. I had no concrete evidence against her at this point, so I decided to keep my suspicions to myself.

George insisted on grabbing one more brownie before we followed the crowd to the set, which had now moved inside the train station. Just as we were about to enter, Nysa appeared, apparently escorting Omar out. "Closed set," she announced. "Only cast and *vital* crew can be inside. Sorry, guys."

Omar glared at Nysa and stormed off, but George, Bess, and I remained standing at the doorway.

George nudged me. "Should we watch through the windows?"

"You can't," Nysa said. "You'll be in frame." With that, she went back inside.

"If only there was a way for us to observe without being in the way," I pondered.

"You know, you can watch everything at video village." I looked up to see Raina walking toward us. She was wearing a tool belt filled with double-sided tape, a lint roller, safety pins, and stain remover. "Follow me."

She led us to a small tent set up on a nearby lawn. Several director-style chairs faced a monitor that showed everything the camera was seeing. I could hear Alex's voice coming through a set of headphones next to the monitor. A number of crew members—including Lali—had gathered around as well.

"This is video village. We can watch and hear what's going on without actually being on set." As she spoke, I could tell that Raina was making an effort to seem confident and poised after the incident in the costume trailer.

"Last looks!" Nysa barked over the walkie-talkie. The makeup artists collected their bags.

"That's my last chance to adjust the costumes before they start shooting!" Raina exclaimed anxiously, hurrying away. "I'll be right back!"

"So what's so intense that we can't be inside?" George asked.

I thumbed through my sides. In this scene, Dylan confessed to his sister that he had amassed a large amount of debt and if they didn't make a quick profit from the Hamilton Inn, loan sharks would come after him.

"That's *it*?" George grumbled. "I thought it was going to be a zombie apocalypse kind of thing."

"Gross, George!" Bess exclaimed.

"*Shhhh!*" came a stern voice from across the tent. We zipped our lips and watched Brian in action.

After the first take, I realized that one of our suspects was missing.

"Where's Cora?" I whispered to George. "I haven't seen her since lunch."

"Me neither," she replied, and Bess shook her head too.

"I'm going to take a quick stroll around," I told them.

I set off, walking from the train station to the other end of the parking lot. I noticed Omar pacing outside Brian's and Zoë's trailers, hands deep in his pockets. He definitely looked frustrated, I assumed because Nysa had kicked him off the set.

Nearby, I could hear Sal grumbling to himself about Nysa's stolen stapler accusation. I was about to try speaking with him again when I noticed Cora coming out of the production trailer with her camera.

"Hey there," I greeted her.

Cora had never been particularly friendly, but the expression on her face made her look downright nervous.

"I was looking for Lali, but nobody's in there," she explained, even though I hadn't asked.

"Everything okay?" I pressed, keeping my tone pleasant.

She avoided eye contact. "I just think I should be allowed on set. How am I supposed to film a behind-the-scenes documentary if my brother won't let me go behind the scenes?"

"Alex made you leave?" I had been sensing friction between the siblings since the moment I arrived.

"Yeah. Brian said I could stay, but Alex thought my camera was distracting everyone from the real camera. You know, I've been studying film way longer than my brother has. Up until two years ago, he was going to be a lawyer!" Her hands were clenched around her camera straps so hard that her knuckles turned white.

I did my best to comfort her. "Well, I'm sure he's just stressed out, what with it being the first day of shooting and having to deal with these pranks."

Cora kept her gaze downcast. "Whatever," she said. "At least Brian gets it, even if my brother doesn't."

She stalked away and plopped down angrily in one of the plastic chairs next to the craft service table. I wanted to linger nearby in hopes of continuing the conversation, but Cora didn't seem to be in a chatty mood.

As I pondered the case further, Zoë swished past me, speaking intensely to someone on her phone. She disappeared into her trailer.

After a few minutes, she poked her head out the door. "Has anyone seen Shea?" she called. A young-looking production assistant with jet-black hair dashed across the parking lot.

"I'm here, Zoë!" he cried. "Sorry! I was looking for the stapler." He stopped to catch his breath. "But that's not as important as you! What do you need?"

Zoë looked a little taken aback by Shea's display of enthusiasm. "I just wanted to see if tomorrow's call sheet was ready. I was wondering what we're shooting."

"You shouldn't be handing out call sheets early," Omar barked from where he was sulking nearby.

"But they're finished," Shea said, looking confused. "Should I ask Nysa first?"

"Omar, don't harass him," Zoë scoffed. "It's fine, Shea. I just need to get an idea of what time I should be here tomorrow. I'm trying to schedule something."

Shea looked anxiously from Zoë to Omar. Finally he said, "I'll get a call sheet, Zoë," and he ran to the production trailer.

"Fine. Don't listen to me," Omar huffed, rummaging around in one of the coolers near the craft service table.

Even though it wasn't first time I'd heard Omar make a snotty comment, he was being particularly harsh on Shea. I wondered if there was something bothering him beyond being kicked off the set.

"Omar, can you hand me a soda?" I asked. "I'm really thirsty."

"Huh?" he said, as if he didn't understand.

"A soda. *Please.*"

"Oh, sure," Omar replied, tossing me a can.

"Are you okay?" I asked. "You seem kind of . . . on edge."

"Yeah," he said. "I'm just tired. The early mornings are getting to me, you know?"

I nodded.

"And I guess I'm a little homesick," he added.

"For L.A.?"

"No, I'm from Vancouver. I've never actually been to Los Angeles," Omar admitted, "but I'm hoping that Brian's next project will take me there."

Shea jogged back out of the production trailer, sweating and wearing a panicked expression.

"Lali?" he called, and then repeated his words into his walkie-talkie. "Has anyone seen Lali? It's an emergency. I need her NOW."

Moments later Lali hurried over. Shea whispered something in her ear, and she snatched the call sheet from his trembling hand.

I leaned over to peek. In big red letters on the bottom of the piece of paper, someone had written: *SHUT IT DOWN, OR YOU'LL BE SORRY.*

✧

CHAPTER FIVE

Double Agent

EARLY THE NEXT MORNING I DROVE BESS and George to the day's first location: the actual Hamilton Inn. We spent the entire car ride going over the events of day one.

The night before, Lali had assured the cast and crew that the threatening note was just another prank, but I could hear the worry starting to seep into her voice. She had already called me that morning to find out if I had any thoughts on a culprit. I had to say no, but I assured her that we were working on leads.

"Shea says the new call sheets were left unattended

in the production trailer for about thirty minutes while he was out looking for the stapler and doing various errands. Someone must have gone inside and left the note during that time," I told my friends.

"But there's no way of knowing if the note was on the call sheet before Cora went inside?" Bess queried.

"Cora says she didn't see the note, but she claims she was only in the production trailer for a second, so it's possible she didn't notice," I responded. "Shea found the note about five minutes after Cora left the trailer."

George raised an eyebrow. "This looks bad for Cora," she said.

"She's high on our suspect list," I replied, "but Sal was also around. And Omar was acting strange too, actually. He didn't want Shea to pass out the call sheets. Maybe he was trying to keep Shea from going inside the trailer."

"Could he have written the note?" Bess asked.

"If he did," I pondered, "he didn't want anyone to find it, which doesn't make any sense at all."

Following handwritten signs that said CREW PARKING,

I drove onto an unpaved road that snaked into the woods. I could feel my car bumping over the sticks and stones as I pulled into a makeshift parking lot set up in a dusty clearing. All the trucks and trailers were parked on the other end of the clearing, along with the craft service tent and its requisite coolers, tables, and chairs. Bess, George, and I got out of my car and followed more signs with arrows pointing toward SET, which led us along a narrow path shrouded by pine trees.

"Whoa," Bess said breathlessly, stopping in her tracks. We had emerged from the dense forest to find ourselves standing in front of the Hamilton Inn, as the creaky, fading sign announced. The "inn" was actually a large, two-story Victorian home with a wide porch, two balconies, and miniature roof spires. Members of the art department ran in and out placing props while electricians rigged lights.

"Pretty amazing, isn't it?" Alex appeared next to us, looking proud. Cora stood next to him.

"The interior looks a little too much like it came

from one of the Harry Potter movies, if you ask me," she scoffed.

Alex frowned at his sister. "I *didn't* ask you."

Cora stormed off in a huff.

George whispered in my ear, "She's not helping her case with that attitude!"

"What was that, George?" Alex inquired.

"Nothing," I said quickly.

"Nancy, I'm starting to get really freaked out that someone's out to sabotage this film," Alex confessed. "It's hard for me to focus when I know that something could go wrong at any moment. Please tell me you've uncovered something!"

"Not quite yet, but it's going really well. Our Nancy always nabs the culprit," Bess proclaimed. "With help from her brilliant friends, of course."

Alex smiled gratefully. "I'll take your word on that."

Nysa sauntered over. "Good morning, all!" she announced cheerily. "Today is going to be a fantastic day!"

Alex appeared amused. "Oh? How do you know?"

"I found the missing stapler!" She held up the piece

of office equipment as if it were a trophy. Sensing our lack of enthusiasm, Nysa shrugged. "We have to find joy in the little things, right?"

"Absolutely!" I laughed. "Where was it?"

"In one of the soda coolers, of all places," Nysa replied. "Sal is such a liar sometimes!"

After a brief pause, Nysa turned to Alex. "Oh, Brian is in hair and makeup if you want to meet with him now."

"Yeah, cool. See you later, Nancy, girls," he said.

"Why would Sal lie about returning the stapler?" I asked.

"Because he's mean," Bess sniffed.

A loud screeching noise cut through our conversation. I turned to see a large black SUV trying to park on the lawn right in front of the Hamilton Inn sign.

Nysa began waving her arms and shouted, "You can't park here!"

The car's tinted window rolled down and a woman's high-pitched voice screeched from within. "Oh, my gosh. I'm *so sorry*. I got incredibly, totally lost!" I glimpsed a shiny golden ponytail and mirrored aviator sunglasses. "Would you mind moving my car to the parking lot?"

Nysa looked taken aback by the request. "Excuse me?"

The blond woman, who looked positively tiny in such a huge vehicle, rolled down her window a little farther and removed her sunglasses. Her face was pristinely made up. "I'm Kendall. Kendall C. Rose," she announced, but Nysa still looked confused. "Brian's agent? I thought my assistant called to tell you I was coming by today."

Kendall looked genuinely upset that Nysa didn't know who she was.

"I didn't get the message." Nysa shrugged. "But no harm. It's nice to meet you. The parking lot is over that way."

"I'm just really bad with directions—like, the *worst*!" Kendall exclaimed. "I'd love it if someone could come with me and show me the way, at least."

I jumped into action. "I'll do it!"

Nysa looked relieved. "Thank you. Kendall, Nancy will take you to the parking lot and walk you back to set."

Kendall flashed her sunny smile in Nysa's direction once more. "Thank you *so* much. That is *so* helpful."

"It's a long shot, but maybe she'll know if someone else has it out for the movie," I whispered to my friends as I trotted over to the SUV.

Once inside, I noticed that Kendall's car was sleek and modern: buttery leather seats, state-of-the-art GPS, the works.

"Nice car," I remarked.

Kendall rolled her eyes. "Omi*god*, are you serious? It was the only one left in the rental place, and it *totally* smells like someone's wet dog in here. Also, what is this color, right? It looks like vomit."

I pointed her in the direction of the parking lot, and she started driving. "So, you're Brian's agent?" I asked.

"Yeah," Kendall replied. "Isn't he great? This Alan Burgess guy is so lucky. You know, I warned Brian about how risky it is for an A-list actor to work with a first-time director. But when he wants to do something, there's no stopping him."

"You mean Alex," I offered. "Turn left here."

"Who?" She yanked her steering wheel sideways, coming jerkily to a stop and putting the car in park.

"Never mind," I said. "So you didn't want Brian to work on this film?"

Kendall opened her door and stepped out of the car. "Oh, I didn't mean it like *that*. It's just—Brian's a star. He can get bigger projects. But I get it, I mean, the whole *Blue Ranger* thing, that was just so . . ."

Before Kendall could finish her sentence, one of her stiletto heels sank right into the mud. "Eek!" she shrieked.

"So . . . what?" I pressed.

But Kendall was preoccupied. "What a mess. Doll, hand me that box on the backseat, would you?"

I had to twist myself into the tiny backseat to reach the cardboard shoe box. On the floor of the car, I noticed a plastic bag with bottles of ketchup and mustard peeking out of the top.

I made sure not to linger for fear of arousing suspicion and quickly handed Kendall the shoe box, which contained a pair of brand-new white tennis shoes.

"When did you get into town, Kendall?" I asked. She changed into the sneakers and tossed her stilettos haphazardly into the backseat, narrowly missing my cheek.

"Oh, two days ago." She grimaced. "I couldn't come to the shoot yesterday because I've had *so* much work to do. I've just been on my phone constantly, trapped in some horrible two-star hotel downtown eating the *worst* food I've ever had."

"So the producers *of The Blue Ranger* must have been really upset when Brian—" I began, when Kendall's phone rang.

"Oh hello, how *are* you?" she shrieked into the phone, pressing her finger to her lips to quiet me. Kendall stayed several feet behind me as I walked her to the set, but even at her lowest volume, I could hear every word. Whoever was on the other end of her call was getting an earful of complaints about River Heights, the lack of good restaurants and Pilates studios, and speculation about what could have possibly possessed Brian to act in such an insignificant film because, according to Kendall, "there's nothing in it for him."

She was still on the phone when we got to Brian's trailer. She barged inside, not bothering to knock. As soon as the door closed behind her, I ran over to Bess and George, who were lingering outside the hair and makeup trailer, I noticed that the trailer was slightly open and inside Cora was filming Zoë getting her hair done.

"Who. Was. That?" George asked, motioning toward Brian's trailer.

"That," I replied, "is Kendall, Brian's agent from Los Angeles and our newest suspect." I recounted everything I'd overheard Kendall say on the phone and shared the additional clue of the ketchup in her backseat.

"But . . . why?" Bess asked, dumbfounded. "If she's Brian's agent, isn't she supposed to be *helping* him?" Bess always wanted to believe the best about everyone, which was part of what made her such a good friend.

I shrugged. "She might think she *is* helping him. She claims he should be in bigger movies, like *The Blue Ranger*, but Brian clearly doesn't agree."

"She'd also be helping herself," George offered. "As Brian's agent, Kendall gets a percentage of his salary, right? If she were to shut down *The Hamilton Inn*, Brian would be free to take on a better-paying role and Kendall would make more money too."

Bess crinkled her nose in disgust. "That does make sense. *And* it would explain why she would be driving around with ketchup in her rental car."

George grabbed her phone and started typing. "Look at this," she said, turning the screen toward us. "Kendall was actually the *assistant* to Brian's main agent and was only promoted a few weeks ago. Brian is her one client!"

"That means that she's dependent on Brian's salary. Definitely a motive," I remarked. "Kendall didn't show up on the first day, even though she was already in town. I wonder if there's some way she could have put the firecrackers in the coffee machine and cut the hole in the wardrobe trailer."

"What about the call sheet?" Bess asked. "I can't imagine her being that close to Brian and Zoë's trailers without someone recognizing her."

"Or hearing her," I added. "I'll stay close to her and see if I can find out anything else."

"We'll stick near the trailers," George whispered. "Cora is still in with Zoë, and Sal . . ." Her eyes darted to the unmanned craft service table.

". . . has disappeared once again," Bess finished.

Brian emerged from his trailer already in costume, and Kendall accompanied him as he walked from the clearing to the set.

I stayed several feet behind them, trudging through the overgrown grass that filled the purposely ill-maintained landscape around the entrance to the Hamilton Inn. According to the call sheet, the first scene took place on the front porch of the house, where Malika and Dylan would be sitting.

Brian and Alex engaged in a deep discussion while

the cinematographer adjusted the camera and lights. Since Zoë was still getting ready, there was a "stand-in" in her place on the set. Nysa had explained that stand-ins are actors who are generally the same size as the stars. They "stand in" so the crew can set up a shot correctly while the main actors are getting hair and makeup done.

Meanwhile, Kendall stayed as close to Brian as possible, as if he were the only person there worth speaking to. I sidled up next to her while she watched her client, full of pride.

"Brian really is an amazing actor," I remarked. "You must love working with him."

Kendall's eyes lit up. "You have no idea, Noreen. He makes me love my job, you know?"

I didn't bother correcting her about my name; there were more important things to discuss.

"So, that *Blue Ranger* movie. You encouraged Brian to audition for the role, right? I don't mean to pry, but I'm such a huge fan," I added for effect.

She took a breath before responding, and for a

moment, I noticed a crack in Kendall's well-groomed demeanor. "I mean, yeah, of course. It was a great opportunity for him. Plus, the studio is hoping it will be a franchise, meaning that Brian could have been in three or four or however many *Blue Ranger* films they decide to make."

For all of Kendall's less appealing characteristics, she did seem to sincerely care about Brian. The question was: How far she would push him along the career path she deemed appropriate?

"But he turned down the *Blue Ranger* movie because of *The Hamilton Inn*," I continued.

"He told you that?" She cocked her head to the side.

"Was it supposed to be a secret?" I asked, surprised.

"No, no. I just didn't realize he . . . whatever. It's over now. And who knows, maybe people will want to watch this little movie. Excuse me." She stepped away and checked her phone, which clearly wasn't ringing.

I couldn't help but roll my eyes.

"She's not as bad as you think." Cora and her camera seemed to magically appear beside me. She nodded toward the retreating Kendall, who was still fiddling with her phone.

"Oh yeah?" I was used to Cora's complaints, but this was the first time I'd heard her utter anything resembling a compliment. "How do you know?"

"She spoke to one of my film classes in Los Angeles," Cora said. "She's pretty smart—once you get past that whole phony act."

"What's the best way to do that?" I asked, confounded.

Cora ignored my question and pressed record on her camera, indicating that our brief discussion was over.

Meanwhile, Alex grew more perturbed. "Where *is* Zoë?" he demanded. "I thought she was on her way to the set like, ten minutes ago."

Brian, steady as ever, replied, "She's coming—look."

I heard rapid footsteps crunching through the leaves behind me. When Zoë appeared, her eyes were red and puffy. Shea followed her, scrambling to keep up.

"I am so sorry for holding you up!" Zoë wailed.

Alex seemed taken aback by her overwhelming show of emotion. "It's fine," he assured her. "Are you . . . okay?"

She clearly wasn't. Shea stepped in to explain, his voice shaking. "If anyone sees a turquoise pendant—"

"I'll pay a reward!" Zoë interrupted. "It was my grandmother's, and it's my lucky charm. She gave it to me before she died. I've looked everywhere. The box is still there, but the pendant is just . . . gone. Someone must have taken it from my trailer while I was in hair and makeup." She choked back a sob.

"What did it look like?" I asked.

"A turquoise heart, about an inch wide all around," she replied with a sniffle.

Brian draped his arm around Zoë's shoulders. "I'm sure we'll find it. Are you okay? Do you need a minute before we get started?"

Zoë shook her head. "I'm fine. Thanks, Brian. Let's just begin. But everyone who can, please keep looking for it!" A makeup artist jumped in to wipe streaks of mascara from Zoë's cheeks.

I wanted to stay on the set, so I texted Bess: ARE YOU STILL NEAR THE TRAILERS? ZOË'S NECKLACE WAS STOLEN!

OH NO! came Bess's response. I'LL STAY HERE AND LOOK FOR CLUES.

As soon as Zoë was ready, Alex walked through the scene with both actors while Spencer made some final adjustments to the lights.

"Rehearsal's up. Quiet on set!" Nysa announced.

Alex threw his hands up in exasperation. "Hey, Cora, want to move back a bit?" he shouted. "You're in the way of the *real* camera."

Cora repositioned herself, but I could see her lips forming angry words under her breath.

"And action on rehearsal!" Nysa cried out.

I used the mandatory silence to think over the case against Cora. I had seen her filming Zoë in the hair and makeup trailer; it was possible that she had been shooting Zoë in her own trailer as well, giving her time to nick the necklace. Cora was also the only person I'd seen enter the production office right before the threatening note appeared. Plus, as a film student she would know how to identify which costume to sabotage. And maybe she had recruited someone else to engineer the fake blood and the fireworks while she filmed the reception.

But as I watched Cora behind the camera, gazing at Brian eagerly, I started to question that theory. Even though Cora had issues with her brother, she sure loved Brian. Why would she want to shut down his film?

My mind was spinning, so I tried to concentrate on Zoë's remarkable performance.

Right after Alex yelled, "CUT!" however, Bess and George jogged up to me.

"Any news from base camp?" I asked, employing the term that I'd heard crew members using to describe the area where the trucks and trailers were parked.

Bess shook her head. "Everyone's just running around looking for that pendant."

"What about this morning? Did you lose track of Cora at any point?"

"Cora didn't go into Zoë's trailer," George remarked,

reading my mind. "We were watching her the whole time."

I sighed. This case already had more twists and tangles than Alex's screenplay.

To prepare for the next shot, a few crew members were placing pieces of metal track on the ground.

"That thing is cool!" George exclaimed when she saw it. "It looks like part of a carnival ride."

"It's called a camera dolly," said Lali, coming up behind us. "I'll tell you all about it for your article. . . ." She trailed off as she led us to the side of the inn, away from prying eyes and ears.

"We need to figure out what's going on, Nancy," Lali said urgently. "These pranks are slowing down the shoot, and a police investigation will only make it worse. We're already over schedule, which means we are over budget. If this prankster strikes again, we may not have enough time or money to finish this movie. I need to know what you've got so far."

"We've identified several possibilities—" I began, but Lali cut me off.

"Wait a minute! Ronan Beale!" she exclaimed, snapping her fingers. "I can't believe I didn't think of him before!"

"Who's that?" George asked.

"Ronan is Alex's old college friend and former writing partner," Lali explained. "A few years ago they got in a fight and stopped speaking. Then, last year— just when we had started casting *The Hamilton Inn*— Ronan threatened to sue Alex because he claimed the story was actually his idea."

"That's a motive if I've ever heard one," I said, growing excited.

"Where is Ronan Beale now?" Bess asked.

"He lives in Los Angeles," Lali replied, suddenly deflating. "Would he really fly all the way out here just to mess with Alex? That would be completely insane."

"I've seen suspects go to much greater lengths to get revenge," I said. "Do you have any way to get in touch with him?"

Lali nodded. "I'll give his agent a call right now." Before she could, her phone started ringing.

"It never ends!" She shook her head. "I'll get you that number in a minute." As she walked away to take the call, I asked George to look up Ronan Beale on her phone. I couldn't help but overhear how agitated Lali sounded; whoever was on the other end of her phone call was clearly upsetting her.

"She can't do that!" Lali hissed. "Can she? Well, fine then. I don't know what to say!" She hung up, and then turned to face the three of us.

"That was someone from Mayor Scarlett's office," Lali muttered. "Apparently, Roberta Ely has filed an official petition to have our shoot removed from the fairgrounds!"

CHAPTER SIX

~

In Hot
Water

AS THE SECOND DAY OF SHOOTING WOUND to a close, the set moved to a room inside the inn. The sun had gone down, leaving a lingering chill in the air. Since there wasn't much space indoors, many crew members had retreated to the warmth of their trailers. Meanwhile, Bess, George, and I sat on plastic chairs in video village, huddled under fuzzy blankets.

Lali had been on the phone all afternoon trying to negotiate with Ms. Ely, but she wasn't getting anywhere. Despite this new wrinkle in the case, I was having a hard time accepting the idea that Ms. Ely was responsible for the pranks. She certainly wanted to shut down *The Hamilton Inn*, but she was pursuing her goal through legitimate channels. Even if I was willing to entertain the idea that she had planted an accomplice on the set to carry out these acts of sabotage, it led me right back to the same perplexing question: Who?

I was also intrigued by the idea of Ronan Beale, Alex's embittered former writing partner. Google hadn't turned up much on him, and though Lali had left messages for his agent, there wasn't yet any response.

"Let's see if we can get anything else out of Sal," George suggested.

"Like more food?" Bess chided her cousin.

"Okay, okay, so our visit to the craft service table may serve a dual purpose," George admitted.

As Bess stood up, George studied her cousin's ensemble more closely. Bess had worn another pastel dress today, but when the temperature dropped, she'd borrowed a sweatshirt from the costume trailer and abandoned her prim sandals for a pair of galoshes, the only shoes Raina had in Bess's size.

"I just realized what your outfit reminds me of, Bess," she said, suppressing a smirk.

"What?" Bess asked innocently.

"It's what Cinderella would wear on a fishing trip!" George snorted.

"Better than looking like one of the pirates who attacks her," Bess retorted. Even though she likes feminine things, Bess is one tough cookie.

"Cinderella, fishing, pirates . . . this is starting to sound like the plot of a weird Disney movie," I said, laughing along with them.

We arrived at the craft service table to discover that once again Sal had abandoned his post. He hadn't refilled the candy bowls either, prompting a frustrated "Harrumph!" from George.

"Nysa to Sal," came a disembodied voice. I jerked my head around before quickly realizing that it was just Sal's walkie-talkie, which he had left on the craft service table.

"Should we try to find him?" Bess wondered aloud. Before we could decide, Shea appeared.

"Where's Sal? He's not answering his walkie and we need hot cider. The actors are freezing!"

Since Sal was nowhere to be found, the three of us helped Shea look for the hot cider mix in his messy van. It truly was a disaster: disorganized boxes of snacks, some open, some empty; a large crate simply marked FRUIT AND STUFF; and soda cans flung everywhere.

"This looks like George's bedroom," Bess remarked.

George scowled at her.

"Hey!" Sal's gruff voice came from behind us. "Get away from my van!"

"Well, we couldn't find you, and Nysa is calling for hot cider on set," Shea said defensively.

"Tell Queen Nysa to be patient for once in her life. I'm bringing it," Sal barked. "Now scoot!" He turned to Bess, George, and me. "That includes you three!" he grunted.

Shea pulled us away. "I think it's best to stay out that angry old man's way right now," he advised.

Back on set, the camera team was setting up outside the front door of the inn. Omar stood by holding a thermos of green juice, Brian's script, and two blankets. As usual, he seemed to be struggling to keep everything balanced, even though I noticed he had started carrying a backpack to ease the load.

"Need some help?" I asked as the three of us approached him.

"It's my job," he insisted, but I could tell he was tired, so I took the blankets from him anyway. He didn't protest.

"Brian is lucky to have such a devoted assistant," I offered. "It seems stressful, especially with all these pranks."

"Thanks for noticing," Omar mumbled, avoiding my gaze. "Sometimes people don't realize how hard this job can be."

"So, is Brian really demanding?" I asked.

"*All* assistant jobs are difficult," Omar said defensively. "But I love working for Brian! He gives me career advice all the time."

"You're an actor too?" I tried to conceal the surprise in my voice.

Omar nodded. "I was Brian's understudy in a play last summer, and he offered me this job to help me learn the acting ropes. I haven't had much time to audition since I started working for him, but I keep telling myself that it'll pay off in the end. Kendall C. Rose knows who I am now, at least."

"What do you mean?" asked Bess.

"I want her to sign me. You know, as a client!" Omar exclaimed.

"But *why*? She's so—so—" George continued to sputtered.

"Hands on!" Bess finished. "She's a really hands-on agent. Is it normal for agents to visit actors on set?"

Omar shrugged. "Sometimes. But Kendall hasn't proven herself in the business yet. Her boss discovered Brian while Kendall was still an assistant. When Kendall was promoted, she took on more of the Brian-related work. Sometimes I think she feels a little insecure."

"Kendall?" Now it was my turn to gasp. From what I had seen, Kendall seemed overly confident . . . to the point of being obnoxious.

Omar nodded. "Especially here. I think she feels like Alex doesn't want her around. See, she tried to help Lali and Alex raise more money for *The Hamilton Inn*, but she fought with Alex when he insisted on hiring Zoë rather than a more famous actress."

"So, Kendall didn't want Zoë to be in the film," I reasoned.

"Not really," Omar answered, "but I think she's coming around. Kendall is whip-smart, which is why I want her to represent me."

"Omar!" Kendall barked from out of nowhere, interrupting our conversation. "You do realize these girls are press, right?" She stared at me angrily. "Lali finally let me in on your little secret. You're a sneaky one, aren't you? Asking me questions, pretending to be interested in Brian's career."

"I was just giving them general information about the film biz." Omar gulped.

"And what you said about Brian earlier is completely off the record," I quickly added. "I promise. We aren't looking for gossip."

Kendall gave me a sidelong glance. "You'd better be telling the truth," she said. I wasn't about to give up on Kendall as a suspect, but clearly I was going to have to be more delicate in my approach.

"I was just telling Omar how perfect Zoë is for this part," I commented. "She's talented, don't you think?"

"Yes," Kendall replied coldly. She gestured toward Sal, who had finally appeared with trays of steaming-hot cider and—with help from Nysa and Shea—was passing them around the set.

"Great. I bet that's made from some supermarket powder that's *filled* with sugar and preservatives," Kendall complained. She cringed when Brian took one of the cups from Nysa's tray.

"Omar, you can't be serious. Brian's not drinking that sludge, is he?"

"No, Kendall. Of course not!" Omar cried. He ran forward with his trusty thermos. Kendall stayed close behind him.

"Omar's trying way too hard to impress Kendall," Bess commented.

"Yeah. What if he's helping Kendall sabotage the film?" George whispered.

"He has a motive," I agreed. "Both of them do."

Meanwhile, Nysa wasn't even trying to hide her frustration with Sal. "Picture's almost up, Sal. We're about to roll and you're in the frame!" she exclaimed.

Sal just kept passing out cider at the same slow pace. "I'm moving as fast as I can!" he fired back, handing off the last cups to two shivering camera assistants.

"Okay, let's shoot this!" Alex called.

"I'm ready, boss!" Brian replied. Even though Omar was waiting with the green juice just a few feet away, Brian took several sips of hot cider instead. He passed his empty cup to Shea.

"And . . . action!"

"I—" Brian started making strange noises. Was he flubbing his lines? Everyone stared at the normally unflappable star. Then Brian started coughing and clutching at his throat.

"Oh no! He's choking!" Kendall lurched forward.

"I know the Heimlich!" Spencer yelled, racing

toward the set. Before he could grab the actor, though, Brian sprinted outside and threw himself against the railing in front of the house. Something flew out of his mouth and landed on the grass, right near where Cora stood.

As Brian caught his breath, Cora held up the offending object: a turquoise, heart-shaped pendant.

CHAPTER SEVEN

Fixed Footage

SILENCE HUNG OVER THE SET WHILE A medic examined Brian. Lali paced, her face completely white. Kendall stayed as close to Brian as possible, muttering words like "amateur" and "ridiculous" under her breath.

Zoë clasped the pendant in her fist, completely confounded.

"I'm so sorry, Brian," she whispered. "I have no idea how it got—why anyone would—"

"Well, I had nothing to do with this, if that's what you're all thinking!" Sal shouted. The light illuminated the rim of his hat, giving his pale, wrinkled face a ghostly glow.

"Sal, calm down, okay?" Lali commanded.

Meanwhile, the implications of this newest prank targeting Brian swirled in my mind: first the bloody sweater, now the pendant. Maybe this wasn't about shutting down *The Hamilton Inn*. Was someone trying to send Brian a message? But how would anyone have known that he would even drink the cider, and beyond that, which cup he would drink from?

"He's fine," the medic announced.

Brian leaped to his feet. "See, Alex? Good as new. Let's keep going."

Alex shot Lali a worried glance.

"I think Brian has dealt with enough today," Kendall proclaimed. "I'll drive him back to the hotel."

"Kendall, stop. I'm feeling great!" Brian insisted. "Lali, Alex, let's finish the day. I'm really okay." He started doing jumping jacks right there to prove his point. "See?"

Brian's antics made Alex smile. "I can't say no to that," he said.

"Alex, come see me after you finish this scene," Lali ordered. "And you!" She summoned the medic. "Stay right here until they're done, just in case. Where are the security guards when I need them? This shouldn't have happened!"

Kendall pulled Lali aside. I inched closer so I could hear what they were saying.

"I think it's time to call the police," Lali said. "This is harassment, plain and simple."

But Kendall shook her head. "Do you have any idea what will happen if it gets out that you're having problems like this? I already don't like those three reporters hanging around! The last thing we need is a rumor that *The Hamilton Inn* is turning into *The Hamilton Circus*!"

"But Brian could have been hurt!" Lali exclaimed.

"That's better than this film getting hurt," Kendall insisted. "If you call the police, I'm pulling Brian off the movie."

"Brian doesn't listen to you, as far as I can tell," Lali sneered. "And don't you dare tell me how to run my set!"

"Fine. Then consider what the investors will think if they hear about an investigation. Pranks are one thing; crimes are a whole new ball game, Lali," Kendall fired back. "Plus, I think—and I'm sure the police will agree—that this pendant thing was an accident. Someone's cheap necklace broke and fell into the cider while it was being passed around. You'll just slow the whole shoot down for nothing. Trust me."

Lali paused. "You have a point," she mumbled.

Interesting, I thought. *Kendall doesn't want to get the police involved.* She was looking more and more guilty by the minute.

Meanwhile, the incident had sent ripples through the crew. Their animated chatter permeated the inn's entrance as they reset the scene.

"All the pranks have been related to food from craft services," I heard Nysa say. "Cider, ketchup, chocolate sauce, the coffee machine . . ."

Lali heard her too and shook her head. "Nysa, that's enough. I won't let this set turn into a witch hunt. Everyone just needs to focus on work. I assure you, I'm taking this very seriously."

I noticed that Sal's expression was particularly stormy, and I figured that he had overheard Nysa's accusation as well. He stormed off into the night. Although the cinema lights illuminated everything on and around the set, most of the lawn surrounding the inn was shrouded in darkness.

"All right, we're going to do another take," Nysa hollered.

"I'm going to follow Sal. I have to find out where he's sneaking off to," I whispered to Bess and George.

"Are you sure?" Bess asked worriedly. "Nancy, let us come with you!"

I appreciated her concern, but I knew that the more people, the more noise, and the more likely that Sal would sense something was off. "Thanks, but I have to do this on my own."

I moved quickly until I was able to identify Sal's silhouette. He'd avoided the well-lit path that led from the set back to base camp. Instead he walked straight into the woods. I fumbled forward, trying to follow the crunch of his footsteps in the leaves until, all of a sudden, the footsteps stopped.

I tiptoed forward cautiously, scanning the trees for movement, when . . .

"Gotcha!" Sal sprang out from behind a tree, and my heart leaped into my throat.

"Um, hey, Sal," I said shakily, trying to gather my nerves.

Sal walked around me in a slow circle. "What are you doing out here?"

"I was . . . looking for the bathroom," I lied.

Sal grunted in response. "I may not be Einstein, but I'm smart enough to know when I'm being followed," he said. "Did Nysa put you up to this?"

"What are you talking about?"

Sal narrowed his eyes at me. "Trust me, young lady, you don't want me as an enemy. I'd better not catch you snooping around me again." He skulked away.

I felt my way out of the woods, trying to wrap my brain around Sal's words. What did he mean by *You don't want me as an enemy?* Was he some kind of hardened criminal?

Nevertheless, he now knew that I had been following him. If he was our culprit, he was going to be even more careful from now on.

When I arrived back on set, the camera was already rolling. Kendall sat firmly planted in her chair, watching the actors closely. She appeared to have recovered from her temper tantrum for the time being. As soon as Nysa screamed, "Cut," I found George, who was watching from video village.

"Where's Bess?" I asked. I wanted to tell them both about my unsettling encounter with Sal.

"She's making new friends." George pointed to a spot on the lawn, where Bess was huddled with Cora and her camera. "Bess somehow convinced Cora to show her the footage she's shot so far, so she could look for clues."

"That's our Bess," I said, perking up. Bess has a knack for buddying up to even the prickliest of characters. "How'd she do it?"

"She probably told Cora she could be vice president of the Brian Newsome Fan Club!" George snorted.

"Okay, this is the martini shot, guys!" Nysa called out.

"The what?" I asked.

"That means it's the last shot of the day," Raina said. I hadn't noticed her before, but there she was, planted in front of the monitors.

"Why don't they just call it the last shot of the day, then?" George asked. "Why make it more complicated? You movie people are nuts."

Raina shrugged. She looked exhausted.

A few moments later an excited Bess motioned to us. We did our best to remain nonchalant as we dashed over to the dark patch of grass where Bess and Cora sat.

"Guys, look what Cora found!" Bess exclaimed.

Cora held up her camera screen. "Last night after wrap, I was testing out settings for shooting in low light. This might explain how Zoë's necklace disappeared," she said quietly.

She pressed play on a video clip that showed the outside of Zoë's trailer. On the screen, someone in a black cap tiptoed up the stairs and into the trailer, then emerged a few moments later. I squinted at the mysterious person; he or she was clearly taking great care not to be seen.

But Cora paused the video on a single frame in which she had managed to catch the person's face. It was only for a split second, but that was all we needed to identify her.

Kendall.

CHAPTER EIGHT

~

Old Frenemies

I DROVE TO THE SET EARLY THE NEXT morning, hoping to have a chance to speak to Alex about our suspects. I told George and Bess to come later; I didn't want Alex to feel overwhelmed. My attempts at cornering Kendall the night before had failed. She had darted back to her hotel as soon as the shoot wrapped.

I parked my car and headed to base camp. Alex wasn't in the catering tent, so I decided to check his trailer. When I got to the trailer area, there was nobody around, but I noticed that Zoë's door was ajar.

"Zoë?" I called. No answer. I listened at the door; I could hear movement, but according to the call sheet, Zoë wasn't due on set for another two hours.

I slowly pushed the door open all the way. There was someone inside, but it wasn't Zoë.

It was Kendall—and she was placing something on Zoë's dressing table.

"What are you doing in here, Kendall?"

"Hey, Nancy," she said calmly, meeting my eyes in the dressing table's mirror. "Lali finally admitted that you're some kind of teen detective after I asked her to kick the 'journalists' off the set. Well, I'm sorry to burst your bubble, but there's no mystery here."

She held up the object in her hand—a thick manila envelope with Zoë's name written on it.

"What's that?" I asked, but Kendall just smiled. She handed me the envelope, and I opened it to find . . .

"Contracts?"

Kendall nodded. "*Signed* contracts. I had to be a little sneaky about picking them up yesterday because I don't want Brian to know that I'm signing

Zoë as a new client. He can be a little territorial sometimes."

So that explains Cora's video, I thought.

"But the ketchup in your car . . . ," I began, and Kendall laughed again.

"You *are* a good detective," she replied, not missing a beat. "I stopped at the store, thinking I could cover up the terrible-tasting hotel food with some decent condiments."

Kendall backed out of Zoë's trailer and continued her explanation outside. I noticed her luggage waiting nearby.

"Are you leaving?" I asked, coming down the steps to stand next to her.

"Yeah. I have to get back to Los Angeles. My flight leaves in a few hours, but first I wanted to return copies of the contracts to Zoë," she replied. "Although I'm still worried about what's been happening here—all the pranks and stuff," she added.

"I'm doing my best to figure out what is going on," I said.

"Well, you can cross me off the suspect list," she said jokingly. Then her tone grew serious. "Look, Nancy. I know I didn't say the nicest things about Alex and the film, but working in Hollywood can make you cynical," she confessed.

"So I've heard," I offered.

She threw me a wry smile. "But from what I've seen, Alex has the potential to be a solid director. *The Hamilton Inn* could be a great opportunity for the world to see what a talented actor Brian is."

"Better than *The Blue Ranger*, even?" I asked.

Kendall shook her head sadly. "I'm not sure what he told you, but Brian didn't get that part. He was so close, but the director didn't think he was right for it. And he was completely devastated. At first I thought he took the role in *The Hamilton Inn* just to take his mind off it. But I guess that sometimes things just work out for the best."

"So he's just telling everyone he turned it down," I clarified.

Kendall nodded. "It's harmless, really," she said. "I guess it makes him feel better."

"I noticed him carrying around a *Blue Ranger* comic book," I recalled.

Kendall paused. "Well, *The Blue Ranger* is scheduled to start shooting in four weeks. I've heard rumors that the actor they cast as the lead is having second thoughts, but it doesn't matter. For Brian, *The Blue Ranger* door is closed. That's why it's better for him to be here, focusing on what's happening next instead of feeling bad about the past."

Nobody would ever know that Brian is feeling bad, I thought. *He must be acting all the time!*

"I should get going," Kendall said. "It was nice to meet you, Nancy. Keep an eye on my clients, will you?"

"I'll try," I replied.

George and Bess arrived not too long after she left.

"Well, I for one am glad to know that Brian's agent isn't trying to ruin his movie," Bess said after I'd filled them in. "Aren't you, Nancy?"

"Of course," I replied, "but that means that our suspect is still at large."

"Speaking of which, I'm dying to know where Sal

went last night," George remarked. I'd told them about my terse exchange with Sal on our drive home.

"You and me both," I said.

Since it was our second day shooting at the Hamilton Inn location, it took the crew less time to prepare for the first shot. All the trailers had remained in the clearing overnight (with ample around-the-clock security), and the inn itself was already dressed and decorated.

"What are they filming today?" George asked, examining my call sheet. "Ooh!" Her eyes lit up. "The haunted house scenes! Lots of creaks and ghosts!"

"That would explain the smoke machine," I replied, pointing at the dense fog pouring out of a window. It made the surrounding woods seem especially eerie.

I finally spotted Alex darting around, talking animatedly to the production designer, the costume designer, and the cinematographer. Even though I desperately wanted to go over our latest findings, I was happy to see him in his element.

"When Alex worked for my dad," I recalled, "he

loved talking about his favorite ghost stories. I can see why he's so excited today."

"Excited . . . and stressed," Lali said, coming up behind us. "He knows you want to talk to him, but he just has no time this morning."

"Okay. Well, in the meantime, did you find out anything about Ronan Beale?" I asked.

"Oh, yes! I forgot to respond to your text message last night. Ronan's agent is no longer representing him, and apparently he's changed his cell phone number. She has no idea how to reach him."

"You don't change your cell phone number unless you're trying to avoid someone," George said.

"Lali, when was the last time Alex and Ronan were in touch?" I asked.

Lali shrugged. "I don't think they've been in contact since Ronan dropped the lawsuit, but I could be wrong."

"What made Ronan drop the lawsuit?"

"I've told you all I know, Nancy," Lali said.

"I really need face time with Alex so I can ask him

about this . . . for the article, of course," I quickly added as I noticed Spencer walking by. He and two other electricians positioned heavy cables along the ground and covered them with leaves. The cables ran into the woods, where they powered a pair of lights so heavy it took three people to lift each one. As soon as Spencer saw the powerful lights flare to life, he doubled back to speak with Lali.

"I need to talk to you about security again," he complained. "I'm still missing my wire cutters, and now my needle-nose pliers are gone, as well as some spools of wire. These are small tools, but they add up."

"All right," she said calmly, "walk with me. Nancy, we'll talk later, okay?"

I nodded, left with no choice but to swallow my questions for now. Investigating a film shoot certainly presented a whole new level of challenges I wasn't used to.

Soon after Lali left, Cora appeared, camera in hand. She had a grin on her face instead of her usual apathetic expression.

"Alex can't yell at me for being in the way this time!" she announced. "I borrowed a zoom lens from a friend! See?" She excitedly showed us her new toy. "It's like spy equipment. I can get close-ups without having to be right on set! I'm going to use it to catch that evil snob Kendall in the act!"

I shook my head. "Kendall left," I told Cora, "and there was no 'act' to catch her in." I relayed the information about Zoë and the contracts.

"Lame," Cora grumbled, her smile fading. "So who are you looking at now?"

"Looking at?"

"Oh, come *on*, Nancy." Cora rolled her eyes. "My brother used to talk about your mysteries all the time. I know you're not writing an article. Don't worry, I'm not going to tell anyone."

Bess, George, and I exchanged glances. It was true—going undercover, especially in a small town like River Heights, was never quite as seamless as I wanted it to be.

"Like I told Bess yesterday, you guys can look at my

footage whenever you want," Cora offered, "for clues or whatever."

"What made you change your mind?" I asked.

"My brother and I don't get along sometimes," Cora admitted, "and it's become worse over the years. But when I showed Bess my footage yesterday, I realized that I'm genuinely excited for him. The last thing I'd want is for someone to ruin his movie."

"That's great, Cora!" Bess exclaimed, giving her new friend's shoulder an affectionate squeeze.

I had to hand it to Bess for getting through to Cora. Her confession seemed sincere; she even let George peer through her new zoom lens.

"I can see Sal's nose hairs from here!" George cried.

"George! Eww!" Bess shrieked.

Even as I watched my friends bond with Cora, I was hesitant about crossing her off the suspect list. Her opinion of Alex had reversed far too quickly. What if she was just pretending to be nice in order to find out how much we actually knew?

Cora wasn't the only one with renewed energy that

morning. Brian arrived in his workout clothes and decided to go for a "quick jog" up and down the stairs of the inn.

"Wow, what is in those green shakes?" George commented as Brian leaped up two, then three stairs at a time.

"I read that Brian ran track and field in high school *and* college," Bess boasted. The word "college" triggered a lightbulb in my head.

"Didn't Lali say that Ronan Beale was Alex's college buddy?" I asked.

Bess nodded. "I think so. Why?"

"I think I know how to find him," I said. "Excuse me."

I found a quiet spot and called Ned. He answered on the first ring.

"I need you to find out about a guy named Ronan Beale who graduated from River Heights University five years ago."

"Good morning to you, too, Nance," came his sleepy reply.

"Hi, Ned. Sorry for waking you. It's just that—"

"Nancy, you don't have to explain." I could hear him getting out of bed. "You think the guy who's messing with Alex's movie went to RHU?"

"Yes. All I know is that he lives in L.A., but then I remembered that all RHU students and alumni have access to the directory," I replied. As preoccupied as I was, it was nice to hear Ned's voice.

"Okay, I'm logging into the network. Yep, here we go. Ronan Beale."

Suddenly Ned's voice became quiet. "Wait a second. . . ."

"What, Ned?"

"It doesn't look like Ronan Beale lives in Los Angeles anymore. All that's here is a forwarding address. . . ."

"Great! Where?"

"It's in River Heights."

By the time I finished my phone call, the atmosphere on set had become noticeably tense. Alex couldn't seem to get the ghost to be as scary as he had hoped, there were issues with maintaining focus throughout the shot, and the entire crew had to huddle in the woods to remain out of frame.

I quickly updated Bess and George on Ned's important discovery.

"Are you *serious*?" Bess gasped.

I nodded. "Well, he is from here. The forwarding address turned out to be his parents' house. I left a message with his mother, saying that I wanted to interview Ronan as part of an article about RHU alumni working in the film business. We'll see if he calls back."

"This is crazy," Bess said. "What are the odds of Ronan being in River Heights right now? He has to be related to the pranks somehow!"

"You girls look way too stressed out!" Brian exclaimed, popping up right in front of us. He had finished with the stairs and was now jogging in laps around the woods. "What's got you down?"

"The ghosts are getting to be a little too realistic for us," I said glumly. Brian stopped to catch his breath and mop his forehead.

"Aren't you tired, Brian?" Bess asked. Apparently she had worked her way up to speaking to him in full sentences.

"Of course, but that's the point. Dylan is supposed to look worn out and frightened in this scene. What do you think?" He messed around, doing a silly *I've just seen my mother's ghost!* reaction, throwing his hands in the air and flailing wildly.

"I believe you," George assessed.

"Of course, if I actually saw a ghost," Brian said, "this is what I'd do." He mimed attacking the ghost and knocking it out with some kind of martial arts moves.

"Aren't ghosts transparent?" I asked.

"Sure, sure," Brian replied. "But what if I have to fight off a snake that crawls out of a sewer?"

"You're crazy!" Bess laughed.

"Brian! We're ready to do a take!" Alex called.

Brian nodded good-bye as he ran off to take his place in front of the camera.

"And—ACTION!"

Apparently, the lengthy rehearsal time had paid off. Everything moved just as it was supposed to. The camera was mounted on a dolly so that it could roll next to Brian as he walked alongside the house, looking pensive. Even Alex calmed down a bit as he watched the first take in the monitor.

In addition to the artificial fog, a creaking sound coming from the trees added to the dramatic mood. I tried to imagine how the shot would look in the final film; the script indicated that many of the more sinister scenes would be enhanced with visual effects.

The creaking sound became louder and suddenly Brian caught my eye, breaking out of character.

"Brian?" Alex said. "What are you . . . cut!"

Before I could register what was happening, Brian pushed me to the ground just a split second before an enormous light tipped over and landed with a resounding crash—right where I had been standing.

CHAPTER NINE

Shadows and Light

"NANCY! ARE YOU OKAY?" ALEX AND LALI rushed over as Bess and George helped me to my feet.

"Yep. A little surprised, is all." I tried to seem composed, but my heart was racing.

"If Brian hadn't seen the light falling . . ." Bess's voice quivered.

Spencer's hands shook as he examined the light stand. "Someone moved the sandbag off the stand and loosened the screw," he muttered. "That's why it fell!"

"Are you sure someone didn't just forget to put on a sandbag and tighten the screw?" Lali asked.

"This light has been here for at least an hour!" Spencer replied defensively. "If someone had forgotten to do those things—which none of my people would— it would have fallen over a long time ago."

"I had to ask!" Lali snapped.

"No, you didn't!" Spencer spat.

"Thank you, Brian," I said gratefully, regaining my balance.

"Anyone would have done the same. I'm just glad I noticed the light tipping over before . . ."

He didn't seem to want to finish the sentence out loud, so I silently added, *before it crushed me like a bug.* Several crew members crowded around the fallen light, murmuring. Sensing the growing dissent among the troops, Lali took charge and addressed the group.

"Listen! Whoever is pulling these pranks is ruining the film and putting all our jobs—and now our lives— in danger. If this is a vendetta against Alex—or me— please have the courage to come forward and discuss this like an adult," she pleaded.

Suddenly Brian was standing right next to her.

"What is the purpose of putting people's lives at risk? What could all of this possibly be worth?" he added passionately.

Lali seemed surprised at first, and then said, "Thank you, Brian. That's exactly right."

As we all looked around, one baffled face to another, nobody could answer the one question that had been plaguing me from the moment the firecrackers went off.

Lali continued, "Alex and I have a legal and financial obligation to finish this film. I will no longer tolerate any of this. From now on, this set is closed. Only those who are absolutely necessary are allowed to be near the inn. I will be placing security guards at the entrance and exit." Lali's eyes were stern; she meant business.

"And I'm calling the police," she mumbled quietly, pulling out her phone. I wasn't about to argue with her. All the other pranks had been startling, sure, but they were harmless. This time, I could have been seriously hurt.

"Back to one, people!" Nysa announced, trying to restore order. George, Bess, and I lingered at the back of the lawn, keeping our distance from the set. Meanwhile, Cora, who had been filming the entire incident, had repositioned herself to capture Spencer and the electricians picking up the fallen light and carrying it away. Her behind-the-scenes documentary was getting to be almost as dramatic as the film itself.

However, when Alex noticed her, he quickly took his sister aside.

I couldn't hear their conversation, but from Cora's reaction, it wasn't hard to guess that Alex had kicked her off the set again. She stomped back to base camp.

"Nancy!" Lali came running over as soon as she finished her phone call. "I'm so sorry this happened to you! Are you sure you're okay?"

I nodded.

"I called the police." She shook her head. "But none of these pranks classify as crimes except for the threatening note, and that was two days ago. They think the rest of the incidents were accidents or plain bad luck."

"Maybe the suspect was targeting Nancy on purpose," George speculated. "Or maybe she's getting too close."

"You may be right," Lali said. "And that's why I need to ask you three to take a step back. Please stop asking so many questions. We can't risk anyone's safety."

"But we can't let the prankster get away with this!" I exclaimed.

Lali shrugged. "He or she may have already done irreversible damage. Our budget was tight to begin with, but with these pranks slowing us down, we've been spending way more than I'd anticipated. I don't think we have enough money left for the big graveyard scene," she confessed. "I don't know what to do. The graveyard is crucial to the film. It's our big dramatic ending!"

"Quiet on set!" Nysa shouted.

"Girls, I'm sorry," Lali said. "You can hang out at base camp, at least until everything has calmed down. Right now, I need to stay focused on making sure that there *is* a movie to save."

She walked away before we could protest any further.

"You know, without the graveyard scene, the Fourth of July Carnival could go on as planned," Bess pointed out as we walked away from the inn.

"That means that if Roberta Ely *is* somehow involved in these pranks," I observed dolefully, "they're working."

We retreated to base camp with the rest of the "non-vitals." Bess insisted that I sit down on one of the plastic chairs near the craft service table and sip water slowly, even though I felt completely fine. Moments later Spencer came running from the set. He was visibly perturbed as he rummaged around in his truck, and when he came out, he was furious.

"Who took my Phillips head screwdriver?" Spencer shouted. "This is so messed up. Come on, guys. I know I had it in my tool belt! I used it ten minutes ago!"

There was no answer.

"Maybe you lost it?" Omar suggested smugly.

"Thanks, man. That's extremely helpful," Spencer

responded. "Seriously, whoever is taking my stuff needs to return it. Just leave it in my truck. No questions asked, okay?"

As I watched Spencer trudge back to the set, I noticed another figure moving through the woods . . . and quickly.

I tried to show Bess and George, but the person was moving too fast.

"It has to be Sal," I whispered. "He's taking the same route as he did yesterday!"

"You stay here, Nancy. Let us go," Bess said.

She should have known that even a near miss with a falling light wasn't enough to stop me from trailing a suspect.

The three of us tried to look as innocent as possible as we meandered around the edge of the woods. Finally we spotted the figure again. It was definitely Sal. We followed him into the trees, taking care to linger far enough behind him so that he wouldn't hear our footsteps. However, he kept picking up his speed until he was practically running; and then he disappeared.

"Oh no," Bess said, peering into the dense foliage in front of us. "We lost him. He could be anywhere."

I glanced at the ground, where I noticed flat spots where the leaves had been trampled to mush.

"Look!" I pointed out. "He's obviously been going along this path regularly. He accidentally paved a trail."

We followed the path of crushed leaves and arrived at a clearing near a small pond. Several feet from shore, Sal sat at a wooden picnic table with his back to us.

"Is he crying?" George whispered, noticing his shaky movements. I thought the same thing for a moment, but then, as I inched closer, I realized . . .

Sal was hunched over a book, taking notes on a yellow legal pad. Suddenly he turned around.

"You again!" he shouted, standing up. "Why can't you let me have some peace?"

"What are you doing out here?" I asked. "You might as well come clean now."

I inched closer until I could see what he was reading: *How to Write and Sell Your Screenplay in Three Easy*

Steps. From what I could see, Sal's notes consisted of diagrams, charts, and names.

"You're writing a screenplay?" I asked, stunned.

"What's it about?" Bess inquired, automatically turning on her bright-eyed charm.

"Very funny. Just go ahead and laugh," Sal challenged her. "Get it out of your system."

"I wasn't joking," Bess said defensively.

Sal narrowed his eyes. "I know what you people think of me," he said. "Just a dumb old man who doesn't know about anything besides milk and cookies."

"Nobody thinks you're stupid," I said truthfully. "A lot of people think you're crabby, though."

"I'm here to collect a paycheck, not make friends," Sal said stubbornly. "And I don't need anyone stealing my ideas." He flipped over his legal pad just to emphasize his point.

"Is that why you're hiding all the way out here in the woods?" I asked.

"It's taken me twenty years of working on film sets to work up the courage to write my own screenplay,"

Sal grumbled, avoiding my gaze, "and I don't want anyone to know if I fail."

He sat down on the bench with his shoulders slumped. "Please don't write about this," he begged, "or tell anyone on the crew."

"We promise," Bess replied, "but I bet people would be a lot more understanding than you think."

"Alex used to be a paralegal for my dad," I told Sal, "and he said that his parents thought he was playing an April Fools' joke when he told them he was going to become a director instead of going to law school."

"So?" Sal grunted.

"So," I continued, "they sure don't think he's joking now."

Sal exhaled. I thought I saw a glimmer of a grin on his face.

"I need to finish my outline," he mumbled. We took the hint and left him alone.

The unexpected discovery of Sal's Hollywood aspirations kept me preoccupied during the short trek back to set. I momentarily stopped thinking about my near-death experience only a short time before. However, seeing the disproportionately large number of crew members milling around base camp was a harsh reminder of how desperate the situation had become—and how far we still were from nailing the culprit.

George groaned. "First Kendall, then Cora, then Sal! We keep ruling out suspects, but we aren't getting closer to the truth!" She flopped down on a chair, exasperated.

"I'm not quite ready to rule out Cora," I interjected.

"You sound more paranoid than Sal," Bess said. "Cora has been trying to *help* us."

"I just don't trust her yet," I insisted. I leaned down to tie my shoelace when a sudden vibration nearly knocked me off my feet.

"What's wrong, Nancy?" Bess squeaked.

I touched my pocket. "It's my cell phone. I put it on silent." I giggled, embarrassed. Maybe my brush with danger had me more unsettled than I realized.

"Hello?"

An unfamiliar male voice said, "Hi, um, this is Ronan Beale. I got a message that you wanted to interview me?"

I had no idea how long Ronan had been back in River Heights, so I couldn't risk revealing my true identity. When I'd left the message with his mother, I'd given my name as Alison. Bess had convinced Raina to lend us a black wig from the costume trailer, claiming that I was considering a "new look" and wanted to see a preview before permanently dying my hair.

Bess walked me to my car, trying to convince me that I needed some lipstick even though I felt sufficiently disguised. However, she stopped prodding when we bumped into Shea pacing near the parking area. He looked sweaty and pale.

"Is Lali down here?" he whispered.

"No," I replied. "I think she's still on set. What's wrong?"

"It's just . . . someone is looking for her." Shea pointed. I followed his gaze just in time to see a woman—the same one I'd seen arguing with Mayor Scarlett on day one—getting out of her car.

"Is that Roberta Ely?" I wondered aloud. Shea nodded.

Roberta Ely stomped from the parking area toward the trailers, her arms swinging at her sides, like a bull raring to attack.

"She looks . . . rather upset," Bess commented.

"That's an understatement," Shea said. "She drove up and immediately began howling about how Lali called her while she was at work and made her come all the way out to the middle of nowhere. I better warn someone before she makes a scene!"

Shea scurried off behind Roberta Ely, who looked angry enough to push down the security guards in order to gain access to the set.

"Lali made *her* come *here*?" Bess repeated, incredulous. "Why would she do that?"

"It's strange for sure," I said, but when I glanced at my watch, I realized I didn't have time to speculate. "I have to go. Ronan only has twenty minutes to meet with me."

"George and I will let you know what happens with Roberta Ely," Bess offered. "Are you okay with seeing Ronan alone?"

I nodded. "We're meeting in a café, so there will be plenty of people around."

"Be careful!" Bess called. I jumped into my car and drove away.

As I pulled into the parking lot of the River Heights Café, I noticed a fit, bald man with round glasses emerging from a clunky red sedan with California license plates. *That must be him,* I thought. In appearance, Ronan and Alex were complete opposites. Where Alex was casual, Ronan seemed formal and put-together. He was wearing a pressed button-down shirt and creased slacks and carried a leather briefcase.

By the time I entered the café, Ronan was sitting alone at a table.

"Ronan Beale? Hi, I'm Alison from the RHU Alumni Committee."

He rose and shook my hand warmly. "Alison! It's such a pleasure to meet you."

He pulled out a chair for me and I sat down. If he was indeed guilty, he was the most gentlemanly criminal I'd ever encountered. The waitress returned with a coffee.

"Triple espresso," she said, placing it in front of him, "and some chocolate-covered espresso beans."

"That's a lot of caffeine!" I observed.

"That's what we do best!" the waitress chirped. "Would you like anything, miss?"

I shook my head politely. By the time the waitress had walked away, Ronan had already finished his espresso. He noticed me looking curiously at his empty cup.

"I'm on this new project, and the hours are intense. I was up all night!" he explained.

"Well, I'll make this quick," I said with a smile. Close up, I could see the physical effects of Ronan's sleeplessness; his glasses actually magnified the deep rings under his eyes.

"By the way, it's such a small world. I realized I'm friends with another filmmaker from your graduating class, Alex Burgess," I began, curious to see Ronan's reaction to hearing Alex's name.

"Alex . . . ," Ronan sputtered, clearly nervous. "You should have mentioned that on the phone."

"Why?" I asked.

Ronan paused. "He's a great guy. Talented, too," he went on, "but we've had . . . differences . . . in the past."

"Oh?" I said innocently, hoping to get him talking.

"Off the record . . . ," he began.

"Yes, of course," I promised.

"Alex and I used to be writing partners. To make a long story short, it ended because I tried to take credit for something that he wrote." He sighed. "I'm not proud of it, but Alex is a better writer than me, and that made me crazy. I would work the same number of hours as he did—sometimes more—but couldn't come up with a single premise. Meanwhile, Alex could generate a hundred ideas in just fifteen minutes."

"That must have been frustrating," I said. "Are you friends now?"

Ronan shook his head. "He hates me. I understand why, but . . . we were friends for a long time before moving to Los Angeles." Ronan's eyes misted over. "I wish we could put this behind us, but he refuses to speak to me."

"Have you tried to contact him since you've been in River Heights?" I pressed. "You know he's also here shooting *The Hamilton Inn*, right?"

"Yeah, I know. Anyway, that's enough about Alex," Ronan declared. "You want to know about what I'm doing now, right?"

"Yes, of course!" I exclaimed. "What is this mystery project that's keeping you up at all hours?"

"I'm not writing anymore. I'm an editor now," he said proudly.

"What does that entail?"

"The editor gets all the film footage from the set, then assembles it in the correct order to make the final movie. It's like putting together a puzzle! After that, we add the music and the titles, making the film look like what you see in the theater. They say that a director gets to make his or her film three times: once during the writing process, once while filming, and then again in the editing room." I could tell how excited Ronan was with his new choice of career. "I'm also doing visual effects, which is something I've always been interested in," he added.

"Are you working on a feature right now?" I asked.

Ronan's phone beeped, and he glanced down to read it.

"It's a documentary, actually," he replied. "In fact, I should be getting back to work now. Was that enough information for you?"

"Yes, thank you. I'll call if I have any other questions," I said. He pulled some bills from his wallet, then paused.

"Does Alex know you're meeting with me?"

"I haven't mentioned it to him," I answered. "Do you not want me to?"

"Oh, no. It's fine. Just tell him . . . tell him I'm

sorry," Ronan mumbled, and scurried out into the parking lot. *He's in a hurry,* I thought as I watched Ronan's banged-up red car chug toward the traffic on Main Street.

As I drove back to the set, I grew increasingly skeptical about Ronan. He was an obvious suspect—a former rival who had been, and maybe still was, admittedly jealous about Alex's success. As Bess had pointed out, it was too much of a coincidence that Ronan happened to be back in River Heights at the exact time that Alex was shooting his film here. Plus, I was curious about this mysterious project that was keeping Ronan up all night. I decided to ask Alex about it as soon as I had the chance.

Of course, when I returned to the set I couldn't approach Alex because he was still preoccupied with directing the first scene. At least there hadn't been any near deaths in my absence. I tracked down George and Bess at base camp and filled them in. They agreed that there was likely more to Ronan's story than he'd shared.

"I wonder if his mystery project is the sabotage!" Bess cried.

"That's what I'm thinking," I replied.

Meanwhile, my friends didn't have anything new to report on the Roberta Ely front; apparently she and Lali had been holed up in Lali's trailer since I left. We agreed that whatever the reason for their meeting, it wasn't friendly. If Lali was simply telling Roberta Ely that she was going to cancel the graveyard scene, why would she want to do that in person? It wasn't like Lali had the time to sit around and have a long chat.

"Hey, Omar! Wait!" Cora called out.

"Is that Omar over there?" she asked as she raced past us. She pointed at the shaggy brown head retreating toward the bathrooms. I squinted in his direction.

"I think that's Spencer, actually," I said, recognizing his black fleece vest.

"They look really similar from behind!" Bess pointed out. "I made that mistake yesterday."

"Omar said he would set up an interview for me with Brian, but I can't find him!" Cora fussed.

"I'm right here, Cora." Brian's voice came from behind us. I turned to see him sitting on a chair several yards away with weights strapped to his ankles, pumping his legs up and down. "Interview away!"

"Oh, there you are!" Cora flashed a toothy grin and turned on her camera.

"So what are you doing, Brian?"

"Just a little leg workout between takes," he responded with a wink. "It's important to keep limber and warm so that I can move fluidly."

George rolled her eyes and under her breath mumbled, "Show-off."

"Cora," Brian said, "I know I've asked you this, and Alex said we had to wait till after we finish shooting, but maybe you can give me some of your footage—the behind-the scenes stuff? I won't distribute it or anything, but I want to show my mom what it's like to be a lead actor in a film!"

Cora cocked her head to the side. "I'll convince Alex and Lali. Don't worry."

"Great!" Brian exclaimed. "It's embarrassing, but

she has been *begging*—and nobody says no to Mama Newsome."

"*Psst!* Nancy!" Omar hissed, coming up behind me. "Have you heard anything about the announcement?"

"No . . . what are you talking about?"

"Nysa just told me that Lali is going to make a big announcement during lunch!" He paused. "I thought that as a journalist you might have some sort of scoop."

"Um, unfortunately not," I replied. "Did she say what it was about?"

Omar looked absolutely terrified. "No, but what if she's canceling the film?" He shuddered at the thought. "Brian's career would be dead! And then so would mine!"

I looked over at Brian, who was soaking up Cora's attention as he talked her through the best ways to get fit while sitting down. If he was aware of the rumors, he didn't seem too concerned. Come to think of it, Brian had been handling all the chaos extremely well. He was utterly unflappable.

As soon as Omar had ducked away to give Brian his green juice, I turned to my friends. "Whatever Lali is going to announce probably has something to do with Roberta Ely," I whispered.

We kept a close eye on the door to the production trailer until Roberta Ely walked out about twenty minutes later. I almost didn't recognize her, because for the first time . . . *she looked happy.*

CHAPTER TEN

Deep Cuts

BY THE TIME LUNCH ROLLED AROUND, rumors were flying. As the cast and crew filed into the catering tent and lined up at the buffet, I heard all kinds of predictions about Lali's announcement.

"I think they're going to shut the whole thing down." Nysa was panicked.

Omar had managed to ease his own anxieties, though. "That's just not possible. Brian would never let it happen," he insisted.

"He's an *actor*, Omar!" Nysa cried. "It's not *up* to him!"

I knew better than to listen to gossip, but even I

couldn't fathom what Lali could have said to make Roberta so pleased. However, regardless of what had transpired in that trailer, I still had to continue my investigation.

Over the past few days, I had learned that the only way to grab a moment with Alex was to hover until he was alone and pounce before anyone else had a chance. I patiently stood aside and waited for him to finish speaking with the cinematographer. As soon as he was free, I ran up to him.

"Nancy! What a day, eh? I can't believe that the light almost . . ." Alex shook his head.

I got right to the point. "Did you know that Ronan Beale is in River Heights now?"

Alex looked at me like I was insane. "Are you serious? Did he move back here permanently? And how do you even know about him, anyway?"

"Lali told me he could be a potential suspect," I replied. "I found his forwarding address in the RHU alumni records. I actually met him for coffee . . . and he says you refuse to speak to him."

"We haven't been in contact since he tried to sue me over this screenplay." Alex sniffed.

"He told me to tell you he was sorry." I relayed the bulk of our conversation to Alex. "I don't think he wanted you to know that he is back in town; apparently he's working on some big project."

Alex twisted his face in confusion. "That is totally bizarre, Nancy," he said. His expression darkened. "But Ronan is not to be trusted."

"I got the impression that he wasn't being exactly truthful," I admitted solemnly.

"Wait, don't move," Alex commanded. "I'll be right back." He hurried over to Lali, who was standing on a chair near the catering tent's entrance, ready to make her announcement.

"Attention, everyone!" Lali said. "This morning Alex and I thought we were going to have to cut the graveyard scene, which as you know is an integral part of the movie. This prankster has delayed our shoot and forced us to burn through our budget. But—thanks to some creative thinking and teamwork—that won't be the case." She pointed to Roberta Ely, who I now noticed was waiting at the back of the catering tent, smiling.

"We will be teaming up with the River Heights Carnival Committees," he continued. "They've agreed to start setting up their annual Fourth of July Carnival a few days early and we decided to use the carnival for our big final scene. That way they can uphold their tradition *and* the film can have a great dramatic ending, even if it takes place at a carnival instead of a graveyard."

The only person who was visibly angry about the change was Brian. He shook his head and grumbled to Omar under his breath.

"What do you think of that?" I whispered to Bess, tilting my head in Brian's direction.

"He probably just doesn't like the idea," she replied. "Not *everything* is a clue, Nancy!"

"I liked the graveyard scene too," George said, "but hopefully this will show the saboteur that it's not quite so easy to shut down *The Hamilton Inn*."

"Or," I speculated, "he or she will try even harder."

"Maybe Roberta *was* guilty all along," Bess pointed out. "In which case we no longer have a case!"

"That still means a bully got her way," I mused, "which doesn't feel right at all."

Despite the news, Lali kept her new "closed set" policy intact. They finished all the scheduled scenes ahead of time and without any unexpected incidents, which was a big relief to Lali and her overstretched budget, as I overheard her telling someone on the phone. By the end of the day, I began to entertain the possibility that Bess was right. With the conflict over the Fourth of July Carnival over, perhaps *The Hamilton Inn* could continue shooting peacefully.

I texted Lali to ask her for a private meeting. I wanted to discuss this Roberta Ely theory with her and put it to bed once and for all.

A few minutes later, when George saw the call sheets for the next day, she let out a yelp.

"It's a night shoot!" she exclaimed. "That means we don't have to be at the fairgrounds until seven p.m.!"

Bess nodded. "So awesome. I love carnivals!"

Meanwhile, Lali had texted back asking me to meet her at her trailer after wrap.

When I arrived, she had the same contented expression she had worn earlier.

"So things worked out with Roberta Ely," I observed.

Lali gave me a tired nod. "What a relief. That woman was not about to give up."

"Was she desperate enough to resort to sabotage?" I asked.

"No," Lali responded. "I even confronted her about it. She seemed horrified that I would ask. The last thing she wants is for River Heights to look bad. Plus, Roberta is all about rules—making them *and* following them."

"Are you sure?" I asked.

"Yes, Nancy." Lali stiffened. "You're not the only one around here who has experience sniffing out deceitful characters. I have to deal with Hollywood studio executives on a daily basis."

With Roberta crossed off the list, I refocused all my energy on Ronan Beale. I finally caught up with

Alex in the parking lot as George, Bess, and I were about to leave.

"I'm sorry we couldn't talk more today, Nancy." Alex sighed as he dumped his bag and folders into his car. "Oh! Maybe you girls can come watch some dailies with me tomorrow afternoon. I'm going to meet my editor at the postproduction facility."

"What are dailies?" Bess asked.

"Just the footage from the movie at the end of any given day," Alex explained. "The actual film that was shot."

"We would love to! Thanks, Alex," I responded. Bess and George nodded enthusiastically.

"We can talk more about Ronan then," Alex whispered. "But right now I have to figure out how to change the entire ending of my screenplay to take place at a carnival instead of a graveyard." He sighed again. "It's going to be a late night!"

"Good luck, Alex," I said as he climbed into his car and drove away. I was impatient to move the investigation forward, but I could understand how anxious

Alex felt about the sudden change in his story. The mystery would have to take a backseat for now; I just hoped the saboteur felt the same way.

That night as I lay in bed, I mulled over Ronan Beale. He truly did seem to feel remorseful about destroying his friendship with Alex, but Alex insisted he couldn't be trusted. Had this mystery project brought Ronan back to River Heights, and did it have anything to do with the case we were investigating?

I also wasn't quite sure if I believed Lali's conclusion about Roberta Ely. I had no reason not to, but something about this mystery just wasn't coming together, and I couldn't let go of a suspect so easily.

The questions kept swirling in my mind, until the effects of the early morning started to take hold. Soon I was fast asleep.

The following afternoon I met George and Bess in front of the Lightning Post, the post-production facility where Alex's team was working. Alex waited for us just inside the front lobby with his editor, Krish, who had a tan complexion and a giant spray of untamed black curls bursting from his head.

"I didn't know you were bringing guests," Krish said nervously after Alex had introduced us. "The edit isn't as far along as I'd like it to be. I'm not ready for an audience."

"Oh, it's fine, Krish! You're always too hard on yourself," Alex assured him. "I just want to see how it looks so far so I can wrap my head around this carnival thing."

"Carnival?" Krish looked horrified. "I don't remember that from the script!"

"It's a new development," Alex explained. "Don't worry, buddy. I'll fill you in. Come on, let's go inside."

"Hey, Krish," came Cora's voice from behind us. She'd just come into the building. "Lali wanted me to copy some of the behind-the-scenes footage to one of your drives," she continued, adding sarcastically, "You know, whatever I was able to get."

She made a point of ignoring her brother and didn't bother to say hello to us, either.

"What's her problem?" Bess whispered under her breath.

"I think she's still angry about Alex kicking her off the set yesterday," I replied.

"That's not *our* fault," Bess said, looking hurt.

We all followed Krish through a set of sliding glass doors, which required a pass code for entry. After that, Krish had to say his name aloud into a small security system with a camera and microphone before someone buzzed him into the main floor of Lightning Post. Once inside, Krish treated us to the world's briefest and most awkward tour around the facility.

"That's, uh, the kitchen. The coffee is good, sometimes. And these are edit suites. I'm working over there. Let me get the key to unlock it. Back there is the mixing stage. For, uh, sound. And then we have some visual effects artists, too, in those rooms. They aren't here yet, I don't think."

He shuffled to the front desk for the key to the editing room, the place where he had been assembling footage for *The Hamilton Inn*.

"Why are we here again?" George was getting impatient. "To look at closed office doors?"

"Don't mind her, Alex." Bess elbowed her cousin in the side, hard. "She's just mad she couldn't sleep all day."

Alex smiled. "I promise we'll make it worth your while, George," he said as we followed Krish inside one of the tiny rooms. Two screens were set up on a desk, with two additional screens mounted on the wall above them. On one wall was a corkboard with index cards arranged on it. Every card seemed to correspond to a scene of the film.

"Krish is an amazing editor," Alex whispered to me. "He takes some time to warm up to new people, but you should see what he can do with just a—"

"Alex!" Krish turned around, agape. "The drives . . . they were right here when I locked up last night!"

"What do you mean, Krish?" Alex sounded confused.

"I—I mean, they're not here!" Krish pointed helplessly to the desk.

"What is he talking about?" I asked.

"So you're telling me the footage," Alex mumbled, thunderstruck, "everything we've been shooting . . ."

Cora blurted out, "It's gone!"

~

CHAPTER ELEVEN

The Full Story

"HOW CAN IT JUST BE GONE?" LALI ASKED incredulously. "How does that even happen?"

A half hour after we'd discovered that the footage had disappeared, Lali met us in the parking lot of the post-production facility. The chaos was distracting everyone else at Lightning Post, so only Krish had remained inside and was going door-to-door to make sure that the drives hadn't somehow been misplaced. Alex was on the verge of a meltdown.

"They can't have gone far," Lali consoled him, even

though it was clear that she was just as panicked. "It has to be a misunderstanding."

"I give up," Alex said, his voice beginning to crack. "If someone wants to ruin this movie so badly, let them!"

"No!" Cora cried in a surprising display of sisterly support. "Alex, you know how hard it was to get this movie made. You can't let this jerk win."

Alex looked at his sister skeptically. "So now what?"

"Go to the set and start walking the crew through the carnival scene," Lali told him. "Nancy and I will stay here until Krish has scoured the place."

"I'll ride with you, bro," Cora offered.

"Nancy, I know you'll be able to crack this one. Won't you?" Alex asked, his expression desperate.

"Sure I will," I replied, though I wasn't sure I believed myself at this point. Lali walked Alex to the car with Cora, who seemed to be doing everything possible to soothe him.

"This is terrible," Bess said, shaking her head. "Nancy, what are you thinking?"

I kept running through the suspects in my mind, but this latest prank was a game changer.

"You saw how heavy-duty the security is here," I said. "There's no way some amateur prankster would risk that kind of break-in."

Lali returned to us and said, "I'm going to call the police again. This time we're looking at a straight-up theft. They'll have to pull security tapes from the building and the parking lot. But what if those drives are really gone? What if they've been deleted? This is going to set us back days. And the investors, I don't even know . . . what am I going to tell them?"

"What about . . ." I trailed off as I spotted something familiar in the parking lot. A beat-up red car with California license plates. Ronan Beale's.

I walked closer and peered through the rear window. There was a comic book lying on the backseat.

"Nancy?" George called out. "What is it?"

"That's Ronan's car," I replied. "I remember it from when I met him for coffee. He did say he was editing something at a postproduction facility, so maybe he's working here."

"So it *is* him!" Lali exclaimed. "Good work, Nancy!" She was about to race into the building, but I stopped her.

"Not so fast! This doesn't make any sense," I pondered aloud. "We have no evidence that Ronan did this. Plus, there's no way he would have been able to target Brian's costume, write on the call sheet, or steal Zoë's necklace without someone seeing him. And whoever rigged the light falling had to be a crew member."

"We always said the suspect probably wasn't working alone," Bess pointed out. "Maybe someone on the set is helping him."

"Or," George joked, "maybe Ronan's some kind of superhero."

George's words echoed in my head, and the pieces clicked into place! I saw exactly what I had been missing all along.

"Lali," I said, "I have to run a quick errand."

"What is it?" Lali asked, bewildered by my sudden change in energy.

"Don't call the police and don't confront Ronan!" I shouted, jumping into my car. "Just meet me at the carnival in an hour! Bess and George, you too! Trust me!"

I arrived at the fairgrounds exactly one hour later, a brown paper bag—and a major piece of evidence—tucked under my arm. The sun wouldn't be setting for a while but I knew the crew would be getting ready for the shoot to begin as soon as it got dark. Although I attended the River Heights Fourth of July Carnival every year, I had never seen the games without people crowded around them, or watched the Ferris wheel turn absent the tinny music and the smell of popcorn. I didn't have time to linger, though.

I easily spotted the film crew under the bright lights and crates of equipment. The process of setting up was much more chaotic than what I had seen in the shoot's first few days.

Lali had texted saying that she was stuck in traffic,

but my news couldn't wait. I quickly ran up to Nysa, who was barking orders at the extras.

"Nysa, where is Alex?" I asked breathlessly.

She handed me a call sheet and pointed toward the Ferris wheel, where Zoë sat alone on a bucket seat at the very bottom. Alex and the cinematographer stood directly in front of her, while Brian leaned on the side of Zoë's bucket, smiling flirtatiously.

"They're going to start shooting when the Ferris wheel begins to move," Nysa informed me.

"I need to talk to Alex right now," I stressed.

"You'll have to wait until after this shot, Nancy," Nysa said. Then a flash of aggravation crossed her face. She yelled into her walkie-talkie, "Wait, why is Brian here? He's not even in this scene. Did someone forget to give him the updated schedule?!"

"Okay, Nysa, we're ready to do a take!" Alex called out.

Nysa jumped into action. Spencer stood behind the Ferris wheel operator, who was poised to start the ride. Everyone else backed away . . . everyone, that is, except for Brian. He was doing some lunges several feet behind it. At first I didn't find his behavior odd, but I suddenly remembered something about the package under my arm. I raced forward.

"Quiet on set! And start the—"

Before Nysa could finish, I threw myself in the Ferris wheel operator's way.

"No! Don't start it!"

"Nancy?" Alex looked over at me. "What's going on?"

"Check Zoë's seat," I gasped. "I bet you anything that something is wrong with it."

"What?" Zoë cried. She scrambled down while the operator checked the bars holding the bucket in place.

"She's right," the operator replied. "There's an attachment loose. But I just did a safety check right before!"

"It's not your fault," I assured the operator. I pulled out the brown paper bag and held up my evidence: a comic book titled *The Blue Ranger: Defender of the Night*.

"It's Brian," I declared. "He's been sabotaging this movie."

"What?" Alex cried.

"I have proof," I said, but Alex seemed to be in shock. He opened and shut his mouth several times, as if he had lost the ability to form words. Lali ran up to us breathlessly, just in time to hear my revelation.

"What are you talking about, Nancy?"

I opened the comic book. "It's all in here," I explained. "He took every single prank from the first issue of this comic book, the same one the movie is based on! And each time, Brian made sure to play the hero," I concluded. "That's why the pranks only took place while the camera was rolling—either the movie camera or Cora's."

Brian, for once, didn't have any peppy responses or inspiring speeches.

"Brian?" Alex prodded. "Is this true?"

"This is ridiculous!" Brian sneered. "A comic book doesn't prove anything. Do you think all these people will just take your word for it?"

"No, but they will take mine," Ronan said, walking up behind me. Brian was now reduced to sputtering.

"Thanks for calling me, Nancy," Ronan said.

"What is *he* doing here?" Alex grunted, clearly not happy to see him.

"Hold on, Alex," I said. "Ronan is actually the reason I figured it out. I recognized the comic book in Ronan's car as the same one I had seen tucked in Brian's script on the first day of the shoot."

"She's right," Ronan said. "I had to move back into my parents' place and admit that my whole writing career was a complete failure. So when Brian came to me with this project, I felt like I had no choice. I thought that if I got into his good books, I might have a chance of getting back into the game."

"He's . . . making . . . this . . . up!" Brian seethed, but nobody was listening to him anymore.

"I don't understand," Alex practically whispered. "What project?"

"Brian didn't work alone," I explained. "He convinced Omar and Ronan to help him. Omar managed to slip the fireworks into the coffee machine when he helped Sal move the table. I'm guessing the argument he had with Brian that day had something to do with it."

We all looked at Omar, whose eyes were glued to the ground.

"Brian promised me a small role in the *Blue Ranger* film if I followed along with his plan," Omar mumbled. "After I planted the fireworks, I told Brian that I couldn't go through with the rest of the pranks, but he convinced me that I'd be passing up a once-in-a-lifetime chance to be a star if I walked away."

"You're lying, Omar!" Brian shouted.

I continued despite his outburst. "When the fireworks went off, Brian was sure to be seen—and photographed—protecting Zoë and Lali. Then he calmed everyone down afterward to show that he had quick instincts and could remain composed in the face of danger, just like the Blue Ranger."

I pulled out the comic book and flipped to an image of the Blue Ranger swooping into a school and calming everyone after an explosion.

I kept going. "In the aftermath of the firecracker incident, Omar stole Spencer's tools and cut the hole on the top of the costume trailer. The grocery bag he was carrying contained ketchup and chocolate syrup. He poured the mixture into the hole, and it dripped onto the sweater."

"You little sneak! How come nobody caught him?" Spencer fumed.

"Because he looks exactly like you from behind," I said, "and I'm guessing he bought one of those fleece vests. Nobody ever questioned him rummaging around in your truck, because the security guards thought it was you."

Lali grabbed Omar's backpack and began rifling through it. Sure enough, she produced the missing tools and the black fleece vest.

"Brian flirted with Cora to make sure she was filming him whenever your camera wasn't rolling," I explained to Alex. "That way he could demonstrate his fearlessness and agility. See, the Blue Ranger can scale entire buildings without assistance—just like Brian scaled the trailer."

I showed him another page of the comic book,

which pictured the Blue Ranger climbing a small apartment building in order to save an old lady trapped on the roof.

"What about the call sheet?" Lali asked. "Does the Blue Ranger write dumb notes?"

"That one threw me off," I admitted. "But then I realized that Omar was also hanging around the production trailer during the time the note appeared. I'm guessing he hid the stapler in the cooler and wrote the note while Shea was out looking for it."

Omar didn't deny anything.

"How'd you figure that one out, Nancy?" George asked, scratching her head and leafing through the comic book. "Brian wasn't even around when Shea found the threatening note on the call sheet."

"I remembered that Zoë had asked for a call sheet early," I said, taking the book back from her. "And Omar tried to stop her from seeing it because he knew that Brian was planning to make a speech when the whole crew collected call sheets at the end of the day."

I flipped to another page where the Blue Ranger

makes a speech to the mayor and his wife, urging them to remain calm after receiving a ransom note threatening their kidnapped daughter.

"But he took the opportunity to give that speech right after the light almost fell on my head instead."

"Did he do that, too?" Bess gasped.

"Yes," I replied dryly, "but I'll get to that. Next was the pendant. Omar stole it and handed it off to Brian, who slipped it into his own cider. He waited for the camera to start rolling before his little stunt," I added. "By the way, Brian, for a television doctor, you should know that if you were actually choking, you wouldn't be able to cough."

Brian grumbled something under his breath. I flipped to another page of the comic book that showed the Blue Ranger proclaiming that he works alone. In the comic book, the Blue Ranger even gives himself stitches after a knife fight.

"But Brian selected a less bloody option," I explained, "and gave himself the Heimlich. The next day he discreetly unscrewed the light fixture and moved the sandbags off its stand while he was showing off his 'frightened' act to Bess, George, and me. Then he made a joke about using his martial arts skills on a serpent coming out of a sewer. That was an important clue. There's a scene in the comic book in which the Blue Ranger fights off a sewer serpent with his bare hands. Then, when he saved me from the falling light, it mimicked a scene in which the Blue Ranger saves someone from being crushed by a falling boulder."

"But how did you know about the Ferris wheel?" Lali choked out the words.

"In the last scene of the comic book," I pointed out, "the Blue Ranger has to save someone else after the sewer serpent pushes her out of a hot air balloon. Once I realized that Brian wasn't even supposed to be here today and saw him doing all those exercises, I assumed that he'd loosened the bucket's nuts and bolts while he was pretending to hang out with Zoë. It's exactly what he did to the light yesterday."

Zoë shrieked, "Brian, I could have died just now!"

"But you wouldn't have! I would have saved you!"

he cried. "I just wanted to prove to the *Blue Ranger* producers that they shouldn't have rejected me. It's been so hard!" Brian wailed, falling apart. "I had to show them that I have what it takes!"

In the minutes that followed, Brian finally admitted that he had done some research and found out that Ronan lived nearby. He then used Ronan's not-so-secret rivalry with Alex (and the promise of a healthy fee) to pressure Ronan into helping him. Ronan agreed and rented a suite at Lightning Post. After Krish left his editing room each night, Ronan would swipe the key and sneak the drives out of the *Hamilton Inn* editing room, copying the footage of Brian's heroics, and then returning the drives by the time Krish returned the following night. The reason the drives were gone that afternoon was because of the schedule change due to the carnival scene; Ronan didn't know that Krish and Alex would be coming in so early. This also explained why Brian kept begging Cora for her documentary footage; he wanted a visual record of the pranks that the film's camera didn't capture.

"Brian, how could you?" Alex said. "Couldn't you just film yourself doing those things without putting this movie in danger?"

"I know how it looks, Alex," Brian pleaded. "But the schedule was too tight for me to organize anything in L.A. I figured I could send this footage to the director and they would realize their mistake by the time we finished shooting. Plus, I would have had the benefit of professional equipment and cinematography. I just wanted to show them—"

"That you're completely *insane*?" Lali exploded. "This is the most ridiculous thing I have ever seen!"

"I didn't think it would affect your film, Lali, I swear!" Brian insisted. "I wanted to show the *Blue Ranger* team that I'm creative and resourceful. I wanted to stand out!"

Lali shook her head in disgust and started frantically typing an e-mail on her smartphone.

"You can still make a great film, Alex," Brian said, falling to his knees. "You have all the footage you need, and I did my absolute best in the role. I mean that."

"I can't believe that you orchestrated every single prank," Alex said. "I don't understand why you would think . . ." He trailed off. "Wow, casting you was such a mistake."

"It wasn't, I swear. No more pranks, I promise!" Brian begged. "Omar, explain to them why I had to do it. You know how brutal this business is!"

Omar heaved all of Brian's belongings on the ground in front of the desperate star: the green juice, the blankets, the scripts, everything.

"I quit," Omar proclaimed defiantly. "I wanted to get a break so badly that I let you convince me to lie, steal, and try to ruin this film. But I'm ashamed of myself now."

"You should be!" Alex shouted. Suddenly his anxiety overshadowed his temporary relief upon learning the truth. "Oh my gosh . . . how am I going to finish this movie now?"

He had barely finished his sentence when Lali started rattling off a list of solutions. "Well, first of all, I can get Eldridge Carter on a plane tonight. He was your second choice to play Dylan, but I know he's still available, so I just texted his agent. We can use some of Brian's fee to pay for reshoots. I'll just spend some time tweaking the budget right now. Don't worry, Alex, it'll be fine." Lali didn't even look up; she just kept furiously typing on her phone screen.

"See"—Cora poked me—"*that's* what a producer does."

"Reshoots? What does that mean?" Brian asked, but everyone ignored him.

Then Ronan piped up. "Lali, you may not have to reshoot anything," he announced.

"Nobody cares what you think!" Alex looked ready to pounce on his former friend, but Spencer held him back.

"Wait, Alex, hear him out," I urged.

"Alex, I only took this job because I was feeling angry and spiteful that you wouldn't take my calls," Ronan said, "but after meeting with Alison—I mean, Nancy—I realized how much I missed being friends with you. I'm so sorry."

Alex's face turned redder than a tomato as he tried to contain his anger.

"Did you say you had an idea, Ronan?" Lali asked impatiently.

"Right. Well, I've been learning how to do visual effects for a while, so I could replace Brian's face with the new actor's in the scenes you've already shot. Free of charge, of course. It would mean you don't have to do reshoots," Ronan said. "Plus, Brian's already paid for the extra room at Lightning Post."

"Really?" Alex asked, still unable to meet Ronan's eyes.

Ronan nodded.

"Let's talk," Lali said, beckoning Ronan over.

"But what about me?" Brian insisted. "I'm under contract!"

Lali gave him a cursory glance and then checked her phone. "Right. Brian, you can discuss that with your lawyer when you get back to L.A. You're booked on the next flight out."

"You can't cast Eldridge Carter in this role," Brian

proclaimed weakly. "Nobody even knows who he is. He hasn't been in *anything*."

"When you finally see *The Hamilton Inn*," Alex told him, "you're going to kick yourself for screwing up your chance to be a part of it. It will be *that* awesome."

After Brian had slunk away in a taxi, Alex gave Bess, George, and me gracious hugs and handshakes. "I don't know how to thank you," he said. "You're all getting invitations to the premiere of *The Hamilton Inn*. You know, provided that we actually finish shooting it."

"I'm sure you'll be fine. You got this far, didn't you?" I assured him. Alex nodded and gave us a friendly wave before getting back to work.

"Thank you, girls," Lali added. "Would you like to stay and watch the rest of the carnival scene?" she asked. "You are more than welcome."

I looked at my friends' tired faces. "I think we're going to take the night off," I replied, "but good luck!"

As I walked back to the parking lot with my friends, I asked them, "So, what do you guys want to do tonight?"

George thought about it for approximately one second before replying, "I'm kind of hungry."

"Oh, maybe we could go to the movies!" Bess exclaimed. "I've been dying to see . . ." She caught herself and looked at both of us.

"Or maybe not," she caught herself.

"Let's save the movie date for next week," I said, laughing.

Dear Diary,

ALEX AND HIS CREW WERE ABLE TO finish shooting *The Hamilton Inn* with Eldridge Carter, an up-and-coming actor, in the role of Dylan. Alex e-mailed me saying that the film is going to premiere at a prestigious festival. Apparently, the critics are already raving about both the lead performances!

Although I'm happy everything worked out for Alex in the end, I wish that Brian had considered how his pranks would affect other people. If he had just relied on his talent, he would have gotten to the top eventually—without causing so much pain. But he had to learn his lesson the hard way—and he lost everything in the process.

P.S. Kendall wrote to ask if I would ever consider turning my stories of sleuthing into a movie. I laughed at first, but now I'm wondering, Diary. . . . Should I answer the call of Hollywood?

READ WHAT HAPPENS IN THE NEXT MYSTERY

IN THE NANCY DREW DIARIES,

The Red Slippers

"I NEED A THING." BESS SIGHED BETWEEN sips of hot chocolate.

"Christmas was just last month. What more could you possibly need?" George shot back.

Bess rolled her eyes. "Not like that. I mean a thing that defines who I am."

"I don't get it. We all know who you are. You're Bess," George said with a shrug, turning her attention back to a game on her phone.

George and Bess are cousins and my two best friends. Even though they seem like total opposites—George doesn't care about looks or clothes, while Bess is a bit of a fashionista; George loves technology and always has the latest gadget, while Bess prefers snail mail to email—they're as close as sisters. Sometimes, though, George can get so caught up in her Twitter feed that she doesn't notice the people sitting right in front of her.

In general, I'm somewhere in between: I like to look nice and put together, but I don't keep with the latest trends; and I like my smartphone, but I'm not obsessed with it. Sometimes I have to be a bridge between them. I could tell this was one of those times.

Bess had been acting weird all day. We'd gone into town to do some errands—mostly just to get out of the house—and she had barely said a word. At first I thought it was the weather—a cold snap had moved in overnight with the threat of snow later—but even after we'd stopped at the Coffee Corner, our favorite café in River Heights and George's place of employment, to get warm, she still hadn't cheered up.

"What's going on, Bess?" I asked as gently as I could. Ironically, Bess is the most emotionally intuitive of the three of us. Whenever George or I are upset, Bess knows exactly what to do or say to make us feel better. I wished Bess could talk to Bess, but I'd try my best instead.

"Remember New Year's Eve?" Bess asked.

I nodded. Bess's parents threw a big party every New Year's Eve. Each year they picked a different theme. One year it was An Evening in Wonderland, and they hung at least a hundred different clocks on the wall, replaced the furniture in one room with doll furniture, spread stuffed bunnies throughout the house, and made placemats out of playing cards. They even hung half a mannequin dressed in a light blue dress with a white apron from the hallway ceiling so it looked like Alice was falling through the rabbit hole into the house. It was always the party of the year, and half of River Heights attended.

George, Bess, and I had been going to that party for as long as we could remember. When we were younger, Bess's parents would herd us up to Bess's room and we'd be asleep long before midnight. As we got older, we kept the tradition of heading up to Bess's room early, only now we watched the ball drop in Times Square on TV, drank glasses of sparkling cider, and shared our resolutions for the coming year.

This year had been no different. The theme of the party had been the 1960s, and George, Bess, and Ned, my boyfriend, had scoured As You Wore, the vintage shop in town, for the perfect outfits. Bess's parents had outdone themselves with the decorations. Entering the house felt like stepping through a time warp. The walls, the furniture, and the rugs were all from the 1960s or earlier. They'd even swapped out their TV for an older model. We ate a ton of food, danced, took goofy pictures in the photo booth the Marvin's rented, and headed up to Bess's room to watch the ball drop. It had seemed like Bess was having as good a time as the rest of us, so I couldn't imagine what would have made her upset.

"Sure. I remember New Year's," I said.

"Do you remember my resolution?" Bess asked. I thought back, but it wasn't coming to mind. Bess noticed my hesitancy. "George said she wanted to crack five thousand followers on Twitter. Ned said he wanted to make the dean's list. You said you wanted to beat your personal record for solving a case."

Suddenly it all came rushing back. "You said you wanted to floss more," I said.

Bess nodded glumly. I could see tears brimming in her eyes, and I felt like a horrible friend because I still didn't know why this was making her so upset.

It was especially frustrating because I'm an amateur detective. I help people track down stolen goods, or figure out who's behind a blackmail attempt. My dad's a prosecutor and he says that I solve more cases than some of the detectives he works with, so I should have been able to put the clues together and figure out why Bess was so sad. I understood that flossing wasn't the most exciting resolution in the world, but it didn't seem worth crying over.

Fortunately, Bess noticed my confusion. "You all have your things. Like George is a computer nerd."

"Hey!" George piped up. She had finally noticed

Bess's mood and had put down her phone.

"Excuse me. A computer *geek*," Bess corrected.

"Thank you," George replied.

"You're a detective. Ned is a brain. But I don't know who I am or what I'm good at or even what I want to be when I get older."

I thought for a second before answering because I wanted to get this right. I finally understood what Bess was saying, and there was some truth to it: She wasn't as easily categorized as me, George, or even Ned, but that didn't mean she had no identity.

"You're the most compassionate and empathetic person I've ever met, Bess," I said finally.